NIGHT SCHOOL

A Reader for Grownups

NIGHT SCHOOL

A Reader for
Grownups

Zsófia
Bán

*Translated from
the Hungarian
by Jim Tucker*

*Afterword by
Péter Nádas*

OPEN LETTER
LITERARY TRANSLATIONS FROM THE UNIVERSITY OF ROCHESTER

Special thanks to Ágnes Eperjesi for permission to use her illustrations in the book.
www.eperjesi.hu

Library of Congress Cataloging-in-Publication Data: Available.
ISBN-13: 978-1-940953-88-5 | ISBN-10: 1-940953-88-X

*This project is supported in part by an award from the National Endowment for the Arts
and the New York State Council on the Arts with the support of Governor
Andrew M. Cuomo and the New York State Legislature.*

*The translation of the book was subsidized by the
Hungarian Books & Translations Office of the Petőfi Literary Museum.*

Printed on acid-free paper in the United States of America.

Text set in Caslon, a family of serif typefaces based on the designs
of William Caslon (1692–1766).

Design by N. J. Furl

Open Letter is the University of Rochester's nonprofit, literary translation press:
Dewey Hall 1-219, Box 278968, Rochester, NY 14627

www.openletterbooks.org

For Hanna, for later

Contents

NIGHT SCHOOL

A Reader for Grownups

Geography / History

Motherwhere

The whole village was in a tizzy. Motherwhere had vanished. Every last nook and cranny had been picked apart, the cellars and attics gone through, haystacks, beehives, pigsties, duck ponds—all checked. They searched for her in the world-renowned peacock-feather collection, all around the vulcanite, in the turbo-incubator (that one had never really worked out), in the experimental drug-spice plantation (that one had), in the cold-turkey clinic, the Wild-Turkey still, amid the black eggs at the bottom of the lonely nest, in the market square, in the market research center, under the slouch, on top of the slouch, among and around the slouch hats, in the ash cans and the trash cans, under the bumps and in the sumps. She was nowhere to be found. The whole village gawked at each other, their spirit broken. She did this a lot. Except that they had always managed to find her, till now. She would always leave them searching for hours on end, delighting in the sheer panic she caused, seeing them wound up, worrying, anxious, fighting, letting down their guard and saying the most outrageous things that even they could hardly believe, knocking each other around, swearing, getting drunk as skunks and giving each other earfuls, cutting in on the dance floor and spitting, becoming too piqued to wait in line—all because of her.

She delighted in it all. But she would always turn up once she had drained her cloyingly sweet glass in the saloon, with two cognacs as a chaser and, with a shame-tinged smile on her face, she would reappear, to a chorus of huzzahs and cloudy dazes and microclimatic solar eclipses.

Kurz und gut, this is how Motherwhere got her name, and also because she had left her position as head of a monastery (and one of the more plum posts at that, which might explain the whole thing),

plus because she could also easily have been everyone's mother even though she didn't look that old and actually she was only mother to one. [Whose mother, in your opinion, was Motherwhere? Argue pro or con.] Look, thought the village whenever it saw her, that's my mother, and extended a greedy hand to her teat for a suck, but Motherwhere would always push it aside since she wasn't too keen on suckling and she had a whole wall covered in notes

to the effect that "my daughter is feeling ill, hence I request to be relieved of suckling for today" and always found a nice, hefty Gypsy woman as a stand-in on such occasions. Which is why, ever since, the whole village has danced like demigods but been repressed by society. For mysterious reasons, Motherwhere wore a large scarlet letter on her clothing, except on Saturdays, when she wore a yellow star, since it went much better with her fur stole. "The disharmony of colors is the death of elegance," was one of Motherwhere's favorite sayings, which the whole village learned just in time. It would never, ever hap-

pen that, say, anyone would be caught wearing red with orange, or tassel loafers with white crepe socks. When the Germans came, the transport leaving the village was laden with a cargo attired in unimpeachable elegance. "I'll gladly die," the village said, "but tasteless I shall never be." Then Motherwhere's chest would swell with pride in her delight at not being shamed by the village's conduct. One must allow that

the Germans appreciated the village's efforts in this area, and indeed they would smack their lips with respect anytime they spotted a tastefully selected *accéssoire*. They had a particular soft spot for hatpins, gold teeth, and refined suede shoes. The Russians were less impressed with such things. When Motherwhere protested as they attempted to dress her in an abrupt-green bouclé skirt with a pink cardigan, which would constitute an assault on good taste, she promptly found herself in the same pickle as good taste itself. None of this, though, irked Motherwhere one whit. She was lovely as ever, mysterious as ever, fragrant as ever, as wretched a cook as ever, as regular a participant in parent-teacher meetings as ever, and drummed her fingers fretfully whenever she couldn't get an open phone line. Naturally, once in a while she would lose her composure, but after all who doesn't, and then she would give the village a prodigious smack that left a welt the shape of Motherwhere's hand on the village's skin

for days. She was always quick to beg pardon, which the village would generously grant. This was the usual game, in which Motherwhere would generally emerge the winner, by the score of 6-2, 5-6, 6-1. The press was absolutely in awe of her forehand, particularly since on occasion they, too, would take one on the cheek. Motherwhere was a real firecracker, a regular McEnroe, howling at the umpire, slamming her racket down, giving the ball boys and girls

a swift kick in the rear whenever they proved insufficiently sprightly. But no one held this against her since no one (and I mean *no* one) had Motherwhere's enchanting smile, or could wriggle their hips as gracefully, or give a flash of shoulder or ankle, or wink as flirtatiously while asking for an appointment at the dentist's. No: the village forgave her for having to ask forgiveness whenever she committed one of her real howlers, because Motherwhere's "nerves were weak" even though, to all appearances, nothing really got to her.

So the village had a fairly wellhowshouldiputit relationship to Motherwhere, but still they wouldn't have traded this wellhowshouldiputit relationship for, say, a domesticated, enthusiastically suckling mama, or a sweet little transvestite running around in an apron, or a mabelnormand, or a motherrussia, a threesisters or a mariecurie, a pregnant she-elephant (even though the latter was decidedly the village's soft spot). Everything was fine just the way it was. Motherwhere was the most motherwhere of all Motherwheres for the village. Of course, for all the village knew, she was the only specimen of that sort in the whole region. There might have been better versions elsewhere, but the village hadn't the faintest inkling thereof. And now she just wouldn't turn up. Motherwhere, who had always turned up without fail even if the village had gotten lost in the GUM department store or on the seashore at Cochabamba, or landed headfirst in a snowdrift, or when it feared it'd gotten knocked up (which was true), or when it decided to be a miserable human being, or when it decided to become a Sister of Mercy (at which time Motherwhere turned up *immediately*), or when it began an incestuous relationship with its father (at which time she waited a little longer to reappear than was proper), or when it was time to turn up for deportation, or volunteer for executioner duty, or show up at the Nuremberg Trials as a simultaneous interpreter (she spoke seven languages), or when she

just had to check in after not talking for a long time because any way you look at it Motherwhere just couldn't go not talking to her village for weeks on end (which in fact did happen). In a word, she had always turned up. But now she was nowhere.

The village was alarmed. It quickly put together a carnival extravaganza, having learned from Motherwhere that when you're totally *verkungelt*, the thing to do is throw a party and invite a bunch of people that a bunch of other people just couldn't stand, then invite them too, serve up the *zuppe* and let a thousand indignations bloom. Ideally in such a situation you forget how alarmed you are because you have to keep the loggerheaded guests at bay, and check to see whether they've started upchucking and whether the police radio was on the air because that's how you found out if the party was really rocking. Motherwhere was an old hand at all this, and an absolute master of etiquette who knew exactly what kind of knife went with what dish, and that the ambassador always drank the lemon juice from the fingerbowls so you needed to put out two of them, she knew that cicadas die quickly, and right into the soup, and that sucking comes after licking, and night after day, and *nao two waiys abat it.* In a word, Motherwhere always said, Don't shrug your shoulders or you'll get stuck that way. Which actually happened. But now Motherwhere wasn't anywhere to let them know. The village was at liberty to shrug its shoulders as long as it felt like it, pick its

nose as far up as its finger would go, boldly flash its bare ass to Pauly Körmendi, poke into others' private business as much as it felt like it, spread awful rumors, point impolitely, wallow in schadenfreude, masturbate (two hands), and exercise its undeniable homosexual inclinations, which was the height of impropriety. [Define "inclination" in your own words. Argue pro or con!] Using the carnival as cover, the village did all this, but felt neither satisfaction nor liberation, and took no pleasure in anything that, at any other time, would fill it with happiness. All of which just alarmed it even more. Now

where would its joy be found, where that glittering wet sensation?

Nonplussed, the village looked at each other and then, after considerable deliberation, hired a detective by the name of Pinkerton who, as it turned out, had a far-eastern woman in the Far East who went by Madame Butterfly; the village found no solace in this fact either. Still, they gave no guff, made no vicious racist remarks, but only stared off glumly into space. They wouldn't have minded if Pinkerton's wife were actually Josephine Baker, though she was a Negro on top of everything else. So the village turned into a liberal democrat from one day to the next, despite its utter lack of interest in politics. Motherwhere had taught the village not to stick its hand into shit because, she said, and I quote, You'll  have shit on your hands. This was just a figure of speech, but Motherwhere was an absolute genius. Still, as the village would later have to learn, there are some situations where you just have to reach into shit (if the price was right, of course) and then you will truly have shit on your hands, but you can get used to it, since you can separate the shit from the chaff if you've ever shucked corn. Pinkerton worked feverishly, observing everything and everyone, taking notes, then providing a punctilious report to his employers since, as later became clear, Pinkerton was (well of course!) a secret agent, but years

later the village wouldn't learn much after requesting his official file from the Office of Historical Records, because Pinkerton's name was blacked out all over the page, making it difficult to determine who the mole really was. The village suspected each other since it respected Pinkerton like its own father, though by that point he was far-flung beyond expectation, and later they heard he'd even become PM.

Motherwhere would have liked Pinkerton since she really went for the tall, dark, and stylish type, and clearly would have tried to talk the village into hitching itself to Pinkerton, who was, I mean, really, a *splendid* fellow and, you see, if the village had come to its senses earlier, then now it could be perched on top of that quaint little trash heap as First Lady. Except that Motherwhere was nowhere to be found, which at any other time wouldn't have bothered the village one bit because then it wouldn't have had to listen to the whole spiel about how it was a muttonheaded little hole-in-the-road and how Motherwhere, back in the day, my God, that sweet little thing whose grandfather had been a rabbi in Sátoraljaújhely for God's sake, all that brilliance together with that elfin little baby-making *ponem*, I mean, how could you *not*? It wouldn't have made any difference if the village had said (if it had even dared). But Motherwhere, if you please, you have to understand, the village isn't drawn to men, you know (well alright, maybe Brando, OK), no, au contraire. Motherwhere would have just elegantly ignored this, or said, with a little performative stamp of her feet, true to the letter of speech act theory: This sort of thing just doesn't happen in our family. But alas, this was untrue.

The village searched for Motherwhere for several more days, then gave up. It was time to face the fact that Motherwhere had disappeared for good this time. Now it had really happened—just like when Motherwhere used to scare the village, but the village didn't believe her because Motherwhere liked to affright the village with the most mindboggling ideas, like when she said the wolf was coming, or that cellulite was about to be made mandatory. Usually the village didn't believe Motherwhere, so why should it believe this now? But even if it *had* believed it, it wouldn't have believed it. That's how complicated everything got when it came to Motherwhere. Time passed, and one day the village was all in a tizzy again. Word had come that the travelling movie man was on the way, and he claimed he had a film in which Motherwhere played the lead. He even claimed that he'd heard Motherwhere had become an actual film diva in some far-off land ringed with palm trees, and had won best female lead

 with this very film. So the village hopped to its feet to go see the picture. It washed itself in a pure spring, put on its best holiday outfit, such as it was (and it was), took a wet comb to its unruly locks, hurriedly slapped on some makeup and giddy-up, off it went to the theater. The village was the first to arrive and so took the best seat in the house to ensure a good view, and waited for the show to begin. The film was

rough going at first, with a slow introduction and voice-over narration, a practice it found absolutely abhorrent. There were long shots, extended takes, desert landscapes, cacti. The village had a hard time imagining how a diva could make her appearance in such a setting. Then, out of nowhere, human figures turned up on the horizon, looking like so many tiny ants, but as they approached you could discern that one of them was a woman waving her arms for help. The village nearly dropped off its wooden bench trying to make out the

woman's features but, alas, she was still too far off. Once the figures were almost close enough to really see their faces, then . . . well then the worst thing happened that the village could have imagined. The film snapped. You could hear the soft clicking of the freewheeling reel against the tense silence. The wandering movie man begged their indulgence, and their patience (patience—can you imagine?) while he spliced the film. He fiddled with it for a while, then gave up. Just won't stick, he said. Never seen anything like it. The village could have throttled him. It moved toward the movie man menacingly, and he, suspecting the worst, ran off. He never set foot in the village again. In its fury, the village dismantled the movie house plank by plank and built a pigsty out of it. This is how the village came to despise movies to the end of its days, and later, when it moved to the city, it still refused to go to the theater. The village never could have survived another film break. And even though it watched the Oscar ceremonies every year, it never again heard from Motherwhere. Now you see her, now you don't.

WRITE A PAPER on the topic of "A Month in the Village." Be careful not to cause a scandal with it either at home or in school!

French

Gustave and Maxime in Egypt

(Or: The Metaphysics of Happening)

> *". . . but an enormous part of our lives is taken
> up with everything that doesn't happen."*
> —Péter Nádas

Gustave and Maxime are traveling. *"Et le petit chat," dit Hélène, "par-tira-t-il aussi?"* Maxime is taking pictures and Gustave is reading. Maxime is running around and Gustave is sitting around. Maxime is enthusiastic and Gustave is bored. Maxime's name is Maxime du Camp, and Gustave's name is Gustave Flaubert. Gustave and Maxime. Fast friends. [Répétéz! Articulez, et parlez à haute voix!]

Gustave is now twenty-eight years of age, as is Maxime. Maxime is two months younger than Gustave. Gustave will be fifty-nine when he dies, Maxime seventy-two. At this point (à ce temps-là) neither suspects this. Gustave and Maxime are traveling to Egypt, suspecting not a thing. Gustave is 183 cm tall, gray-green eyes, attractive, and cuts a fine figure indeed. He has a beard and mustache. He claims to be of Iroquois extraction, which makes him immediately sympatico in the eyes of many. Here is what Maxime relates about Gustave forty years later.

Traduisez!

"He was an exceptionally beautiful boy . . . the white skin of his cheeks danced with rose-pink, and with his shock of hair, his striking mien, broad shoulders, thick golden beard, large sea-green eyes

shadowed by deep black lashes, his resonant trumpet of a voice, exuberant gestures, and swelling laughter made of him the image of a young Gallic general in arms against the Roman legions."

Maxime is an industrious and nimble boy. He takes more than 25,000 calotypes on this trip. This is what Maxime looked like before their departure:

As for Gustave, we don't know what he looked like before their departure.

Upon their return (1851), Maxime has one photo album and one trip diary published. Not one of the published images portrays Gustave. Not one of the entries in the trip diary mentions Gustave. [Qu'en pensez-vous?]

Upon their return (1851), Gustave publishes nothing. Upon their return, Gustave begins writing a novel. The title of the novel is *Madame Bovary*. Later, Gustave would make a fascinating declaration that he himself was Madame Bovary. [Expliquez!] Maxime is not mentioned in the novel even once.

Maxime wears a Renaissance ring with a cameo of a satyr. He had given this to Gustave five years before their voyage. In return, Gustave gives Maxime a signet ring on which he had Maxime's initials engraved and a slogan whose text is unknown to us. It was a sort of intellectual proposal of marriage, Maxime would later write.

Gustave writes diligently, keeping to a schedule. Eight months before their voyage, on the night of February 13-14, he writes the following in his notebook:

"One can do so very much in a single evening. After dinner, I conversed with my mother, then dreamt of travels and possible lives. I wrote almost one whole chorus of *St. Anthony* (the dog-headed-monkeys part), read the entire first volume of *Memoirs from Beyond the Grave*, then smoked three pipes, and now, take a pill. After that, a shit. And sleep is still far off!"

Gustave muses incessantly about the Grand Voyage. Alas, there is no chance his mother would allow him on such a perilous undertaking to the ends of the earth. One example why: In September of 1846, Gustave's mother stands white as a sheet on the platform of the train station where the 25-year-old Gustave returns, one day later than promised. Gustave then renounces all further nights that were to have been spent with his beloved, Louise Colet. My mother needs me, explains Gustave to Louise. "As we know," explains crackerjack Flaubert scholar Jean-Pierre, "this unusual situation gave rise to one of the most sublime epistolary correspondences in French literature." *Merci, Madame Flaubert, merci à vous!* Alternately: Thank you, dear Louise, for you have the patience of an angel.

Jean-Pierre delivers his lectures in a stunning sky-blue jacket over

a wispy, pale-pink shirt. *Le jour de gloire est arrivé!* I would softly add, in admiration, just for the sake of objectivity. Objectivity is the main thing in scholarship. Objectively speaking, there are two sorts of people: the ones who know they are prudes, and the ones who don't know they are prudes. Jean-Pierre, for example, doesn't know. But still, he is. This is what makes scholarship so wonderful. Jean-Pierre loves three things: 1) Himself, 2) Flaubert, and 3) Women. In that order. Jean-Pierre also likes men, but that is not on this list.

[Question: Is it on any list?]

On the last day of April 1849, the widow Mrs. Flaubert (residing at 7 Rue des Beauxjours, Croisset) collapses under the weight of the reasoning of Maxime de Camp, Achille Flaubert, and Dr. Cloquet. *Crack.* Well if there's nothing else for Gustave's health, then fine, let

him voyage to the East. If it must be, then let what must happen, happen. But did what had to happen really happen? And perchance is what happens more important than all that does not happen? [*Qu'en pensez-vous?*]

Before the voyage, Maxime resolves that he will (*futur dans le passé!*), in revolutionary fashion (*technologie moderne*) and "with utmost fidelity" document it through photographs. But the unexpected revelatory force of the images proves on occasion to shake him to his very core. At such times, he rips them up. (Exposure time: min. 2 mins.; destruction time: max. 1 min.)

After the voyage, Gustave resolves he will (*f. dans le p.*), in revolutionary fashion (*style moderne*) write in suitable language and "with utmost fidelity." Still, there are certain words (*le mot juste*) that, on occasion, shake him, too, to his very core. When this occurs, he erases. (Exposure time: max. 2 nanoseconds.) After all, let the *juste* have its limits (*subjonctif*) too!

The deletions are clearly discernable in the manuscripts, to which Jean-Pierre, chic scholar of deletion, has devoted his career. Ah, to fiddle with the deletions of others, and poke about in the discovery of unhappened happenings! *Que c'est bizarre, que c'est étrange!* This is said to be the very pinnacle of repressive effect inasmuch as, *chemin faisant*, there is no

time for the examination of self-deletions. Between deletions, Jean-Pierre likes to screw; he says this relaxes him. *Je*, as a student of French, offer assistance in pursuit of excellence. Jean-Pierre prefers it from behind (see also Huysmans's *A rebours*), which helps the Flaubert go more smoothly the following day. I let him. After all, I love literature.

Gustave and Maxime set out in October of 1849. Maxime is jubilant. Gustave is swept on a tide of ecstasy (see also the widow Flaubert's last words: "Are you trying to kill me, Gus?!") For me, writes Gustave, friendship is like a camel. Once it gets going, nothing can stop it. Gustave is mistaken. There are some things that can (pronounced *Cannes*).

Travel is the greatest enemy of a friendship. Or perhaps not. But if it is, then it goes whole hog. Gustave is bored. Gustave is not the least interested in fulfillment. Maxime is astonished by this, yet remains displeased. Gustave, chuffs Maxime, is just like Honoré: he looks at nothing but remembers everything. But who wants to climb up to the guano-caked attic of fulfillment, thinks Gustave. Gustave is no devoté of unnecessary exertion. Gustave is phenomenally corpulent. Gustave is cantilevered to the top of the Great Pyramid by twelve Arab servants. At the peak of the Great Pyramid,

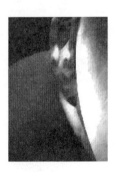

gasping for air, they have a look around. The Pharaoh can just suck all my dicks, thinks Gustave. *Le sport aide non seulement le développement physique, mais aussi la formation morale* (Baron Pierre de Coubertin, *Les jeux Olympiques*). [Mémorisez!]

". . . dear God, what is this constant exhaustion that weighs me down wherever I go! It even accompanies me on my trip! It has become one with me! Deianeira's shirt did not cling to Hercules' shoulders any more fiercely than this boredom to my life! The only difference is, it kills more slowly! It's Monday. The Khamsin is blustering, the clouds are red . . ." [Traduisez!]

The Khamsin is blustering. Gustave is blustering. Gustave finds a white chameleon. Maxime strikes it dead. Gustave spots a flying heron. Maxime shoots it. Gustave and Maxime's eyes meet. Their chests heave. Those sea-green eyes, those black lashes. [Deleted] Gustave and Maxime walk through the desert. Gustave and Maxime have been walking through the desert for three days without a drop of water.

Dialogue:

G: Remember the lemon ice we had at Tortini's?

M: (nods)

G: Lemon ice is just heavenly. Admit it, you'd love to toss back a lemon ice right now.

M: Indeed I would.

(Five minutes later)

G: Oh, those lemon ices! The steam that envelops the cup like a white jelly.

M: Could we change the subject?

G: That would be nice, but lemon ice is clearly worthy of having its praises sung. Take a spoonful and there it towers like a little cathedral; gently spread it between tongue and palate. As it slowly melts, it exudes a fresh, magnificent savor, bathing the uvula, gently stroking the tonsils, sliding down the esophagus (to the latter's boundless delight), and then it reaches the stomach, which veritably cackles in glee. Just between us, a lemon ice is just what the Kusheir Desert needs!

M: (silence)

G: Lemon ice! Lemon ice!

M: (I'm going to kill him.)

Maxime kills Gustave. World literature mourns. At this point,

Gustave hasn't even written *Madame Bovary*. All right then, sighs Maxime. I'll spare him. I can use this one later (which he did). He rewrites the end of the scene, like this:

G: My dear Max, thank you ever so much for not shooting me in the head. I'd have done it if I were you.

M: Gustave, this could be the beginning of a beautiful friendship.

(FIN)

Gustave and Maxime go whoring. Gustave still has some of that fine sausage from home, as well as a case of *morbus gallicus*. *Non, je ne regrette rien!* Secretly, Maxime is fascinated by him, and jealous.

"I go off with that dissolute Safia-Zugera, a rakish little tigress. I sully the settee." Gustave has an obsessional neurosis. He cannot stand disorder.

"During my second round with Kücsük, when I kissed her on the shoulder and felt her round choker under my teeth, her pussy like a stained velvet pillow, I was a wild animal."

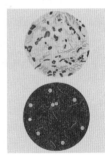

Here the student of French will respond: "Jean-Pierre, *mon cher*, that phrase, 'stained velvet pillow'—would you call it adjectival or verbal?" [Qu'en pensez-vous?]

Louise Colet's reaction: "Gustave, you bastard, go get fucked!" (Which he did.)

Hassan el-Bilbezi: a dancer dressed as a woman. "His belly and hips gyrate hypnotically—the belly veritably undulates—and during the grand finale, his pantaloons inflate and open." [Deleted]

Gustave and Maxime look at each other with some surprise. As if Gustave were seeing Maxime for the very first time. ". . . What is his name, where could he be living, what about his life, or his past? He would have liked to explore the furnishings in Maxime's room, every

 last article of his clothing, the people he sees. The desire for physical possession disappeared behind a deeper curiosity, an excruciating curiosity that knew no bounds." [Gustave deletes this remark, and uses it elsewhere. Jean-Pierre mentions nothing of this.] Gustave has a thought: travel is a sentimental education. This pleases him and he writes it down.

Gustave and Maxime draw their voyage to a close. They smoke a water pipe in a Greek café. Later, Gustave writes about it all, surprisingly, elsewhere. [Jean-Pierre is silent on this.]:

"He took a trip. He came to know, one after the other, the melancholy of great ships, the shiver of awakening in a desert tent, the sweet lulling intoxication of those landscapes and ruins, and the strange bitterness of shattered temptation."

And then: "A miserable attack of nerves about three in the afternoon." [Jean-Pierre at last reports, in a footnote: "It is quite difficult to make out these words, overwritten in a light blue ink; the deletions only serve to render the text unreadable. This is not the result of the author's corrections but rather the bowdlerizations of Caroline Franklin-Grout." Caroline is Gustave's niece. She manages Gustave's papers. Caroline is an impossible prude. "The text, then, is unreadable," continues a triumphant Jean-Pierre, "but the word 'nerves' glows faintly through the ink. It appears that the word 'seizure' follows it."

Jean-Pierre has exposed Caroline. Jean-Pierre is not fond of Caroline.

[Répétez!]

O Caroline, O Jean-Pierre!

The word "nerves" glows faintly through the ink.

Chemistry /
Physical Education

What Is This Thing Called the Exchange Reaction?

(destructive affinities)

"mehr licht"

Their hair, their T-shirt, their shoelaces—all frayed. They are playing ping-pong. It's a heated match, as there are stakes involved. The players: Charlotte (Shatzi to her friends), Edward (Dudi), Ottilia (Oti), and Otto (the Captain). This little company is known in their circles as the Control Group. The game has been going for hours; their backs are soaked in perspiration. On this side, a serve; on the other, a switch.

They have a good chemistry going, thinks Dudi. When he strikes the ball, his eyes narrow to a slit. He hits it as if there were much at stake. He hits it so it hurts. Goddammit, Shatzi, says Dudi, don't sneak up on me while I'm serving. Now he's getting aggravated. Very aggravated. They are the unbeatable team in the Control Group, the

 ideal doubles partners, the dynamic duo. And here comes this pain-in-the-ass with his little stray, looking to pound them. And it's working. Concentrate, dammit! Can't have the Captain walking all over us, especially with that little loudmouth too. He sure can pick 'em. Next time he'll show up with a nun. She's really getting to me with that inquisitive little smile on her face. Makes you think twice about cussing in

front of her. How can you keep your eyes on the ball when you can't get your mind off your cock? Alright. Who gives a shit? She can just get used to it, and be grateful if we let her in. *If.* Because that might still be a while. The Baroness takes a pretty dim view of her, and once the Baroness gets her teeth into you, you're down for the count. Of course the Baroness is fifty and takes a pretty dim view of everyone who's under 30 and female. I like the Captain, but if things go too far I'll be telling him to take that little tease grazing someplace else. Just get her to stop staring with those big, brown, puppy-dog eyes. Really getting on my nerves. They're up 11-6. Not good. Net! Dammit.

Hm, thinks Shatzi. *Apparently* they've got chemistry. They play together pretty well, but are they right for each other, I dunno. Nicked the edge! Finally luck is on my side, so so *very* sorry my dears. They're both precise and well-groomed, which of course helps them coordinate their play. Still that little girl is kind of fishy, as if on the verge of exploding if mixed into certain chemical solutions, but up until then seems completely harmless. Inasmuch as everything relates to itself in some way, so it must be the same with others. And given the differences between beings, this relation cannot but vary. It goes without saying that the complicated cases are the most interesting ones, and the only ones that instruct us about the various levels of relationship: close, or intense, or distant, or superficial. The

most fascinating are those that end in breakups. Serve here, switchover there! Those two are on the verge of winning this one. Dudi, clearly ecstatic, has still managed to keep his composure pretty well. An angry hothead can be so pathetic, but those teary-eyed men—well, they are the good ones. Partners who bring on split-ups used to be called breakup artists. How charming. But actually it is unification that is an art, an achievement. I mean, who doesn't know how to split up? Just a matter of putting your back into it. Now the Captain and his little favorite are constantly sizing me up, which gets on my nerves. They both have those big, brown, puppy-dog eyes. Funny. Or maybe it's not their eyes but something else they have in common? But what? Well, alright, they took that first one 21-18. And we'd made up a lot of ground too. But now Dudi's constant bluster is upsetting my concentration. And something else, too. But what?

Our chemistry is good, thought the Captain, but is that enough for happiness? Just as everything relates to itself in some fashion, so it must to other things. And given the differences between beings, this relationship cannot but vary. Sometimes friends and old acquaintances meet, and unite in no time at all without altering anything in one another, like wine mixing with water. Yet aren't wine and water—separately—nobler than a spritzer? Now *there's* a creampuff shot! We're up 1-0. But (and herein lies the real issue) is there any need for a unification that gives rise to nothing new? Do we  really wish nothing, no one, to change us in the least? Can we really be so misguided as to claim perfection? So averse to change? Is it not change itself that makes our lives bearable? Change that casts us into time instead of running around in circles, making existence something we can feel? If we awaken to the same day each morning, would death not be preferable? Oti and I came together swiftly, without a hitch, like wine and water, and all that came of it was a watered-down spritzer. Net! I always say we should draw a clear line between work and life. Work demands seriousness and discipline, but  life requires caprice. Life demands a focused consistency, but life needs inconsistency—indeed, inconsistency is lovable, even joyful. If you are certain in the one, you will be that much more liberated in the other, instead of having freedom sweep you away in the process of synthesis, annihilating any certainties. And there is no one more consistent while at work than me. So as for life, bring on the whimsy, bring on freedom! This little filly is a tasty morsel, but the real delicacy, the real challenge is pulsating there, across the net, like a shimmering mirage. I must have her. That will be my lovable inconsistency. Smash! We're up 6-4. Serve here, switchover there.

No doubt about it, our chemistry is good, muses Oti, squinting at the Captain. We've got the crucial affinity, that elemental, spiritual kinship, more than we should, even. We both want the same thing— too much, even. I knew a girl like that back at St. Regina's. At first

we were bosom buddies and adored that oneness, the image of ourselves in the other. We did everything together, all that was permitted and all that was forbidden. But after a time we meant no more to each other than wallpaper to a wall. We lacked that spark that would have ignited something new, something different. For how can your character, your individuality, stand up against your way of life, when it is precisely that very way of life that should enhance your character? Everyone would like to be meaningful, just not at the cost of discomfort. Well, I'm prepared to accept such discomfort! This is exactly what I understood when I—quite unexpectedly for myself—returned Dudi's slam. What a man! We never drift so far from our desires as to imagine that what we long for is ours. What's more, no one is more a slave than the one who considers himself free without actually being so. Furthermore, we generally imagine people to be more dangerous than they truly are. Moreover, "it is the mark of a motley, dissipated sort of life, to be able to endure monkeys, and parrots, and black people, about one's self.

Many times when a certain longing curiosity about these strange objects has come over me, I have envied the traveler who sees such marvels in living, every-day connection with other marvels. But he, too, must have become another man. Palm-trees will not allow a man to wander among them with impunity; and

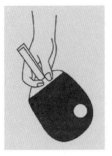

doubtless his tone of thinking becomes very different in a land where elephants and tigers are at home."

Oti looks up across the net. The Captain is a pretty good catch, but the real delicacy, the real challenge is pulsating over across the net like a shimmering mirage. I must have her. We never drift farther from our desires than would let us imagine that what we long for is ours. I don't imagine this, rather, I *know* that it will be. And with that, a forehand puts the ball on the far right corner. We're up 15-13, *salve regina*.

We've got good chemistry, thinks Dudi. No two ways about it: she's fixated on me, ever eyeballing me with those gorgeous, brown, puppy-dog eyes, returning my smashes out of nowhere, and respecting me for being such a man. She's a pretty little girl in fact. Sweet little doofy smile. When you're talking to her you think twice about what you're saying; it doesn't feel right to cuss within her earshot. This is a new one on me, and a tad worrisome. I might even let her have a look at the book from which I happen to be reading aloud. I never let Shatzi look, since it's such an irritating practice. But still. Those two are just about to win the second game too, but somehow that doesn't irritate me enough. Sluggishness of the spirit or something, but whatever it is, it's ruining my game. I'm making some absolutely horrible shots, it's a wonder Shatzi isn't yelling at me yet. But seems like she's in an unusually understanding mood too.

Never seen her like that. A little strange. They're up 18-15. Why doesn't this bother me? My God, give some sign to your poor, confused player. Double fault! Damn it! But in the end, who cares? I'm happy. Unfathomably, boundlessly happy.

If I'm not mistaken, and we know I'm never mistaken, our chemistry is particularly good, thinks Shatzi. Seeing her husband satisfied she, too, sees the rewards of the new situation. Some people, like Dudi, cultivate their gardens and others, like me, create parks or new

projects, thinks Shatzi, topping her mature forehand with another point. There'll be more points coming, just wait till it's over. Serve here, switchover there. This match is a bigger challenge than I expected, and now all I want is to finish it off. Actually, I've never wanted anything more. The Control Group is going to lose its mind, that's for sure, but strangely this causes me neither joy nor regret. Only one thing interests me, and that is to turn this chemistry into biology. We might lose this game, but the match, well, that will be mine.

The Captain exults: No one, not even a blind man, can deny our wonderful chemistry! I've never seen her so fresh, so happy. What else could be the cause but the tension that arcs between us, separated only by a flimsy little net? What else could have made her face bloom like this, make her tremble with excitement, set her entire being aglow, but the shores of bliss reflecting the dawn, far beyond the net, beyond the match, even beyond the Control Group, illuminating an entire life. How could I have been so blind as to miss the solution that was my sole salvation? How could I not realize that *nomen est omen*: that I can be the Captain only of my own heart and nothing else? It took a little innocent ping-pong for me to awaken to what I should have always known. I was blind, and only thought I saw. We always imagine that we see, no matter the situation. I believe men dream only so they may not cease to see.

But there is one thing we do not see, and that is our own blindness. Now that this realization has come to me, all else I have ever wanted only unconsciously can be mine as well. So time to put an end to all this foreplay and see what comes next. We're up 20-19, now comes game and match point. Yesss! Thanks very much for the game, and now, *endlich*, bring on real life!

I feel that there is good chemistry between us, says Oti in a pale whisper; Shatzi nods. Feelings become very different in a land where elephants and tigers are at home.

Shatzi and Oti draw close, side by side, and make their way to the pub. Dudi and the Captain remain behind, watching them. "Nothing short of an infinite endurance would be enough, and easy and contented as he was, what could he know of an infinite agony? There are cases," he continued, "yes, there are, where comfort is a lie, and despair is a duty. Go, heap your scorn upon the noble Greek, who well knows how to delineate heroes, when in their anguish he lets those heroes weep. He has even a proverb, 'Men who can weep are good / Leave me, all you with dry heart and dry eye. Curses on the happy, to whom the wretched serve but for a spectacle. When body and soul are torn in pieces with agony, they are to bear it—yes, to be noble and bear it, if they are to be allowed to go off the scene with applause. Like the gladiators, they must die with dignity before the eyes of the multitude,'" thinks Dudi, but ultimately all he 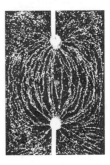 says is, The beer is on me. Every trace of the unpleasant, ungracious feelings of the intervening time had vanished. No one had any secret complaint against another; there were no cross purposes, no bitterness. All that remains is sorrow perching on their shoulders like a great black bird. The Captain gives a resigned nod. They are on the same page. Victory and defeat. Words.

1) Have you ever experienced an exchange reaction at home? If so, how did you protect yourselves from it?`

2) Is it permissible for a lady chemistry teacher to scrunch up her eyes and say, I just *lurve* you my little bunnies? Can this be tolerated?

Health / Homeland

The Two Fridas

(school beyond the border)

They had us sitting together, though that wasn't what we wanted. We even said we didn't. At that, our teacher whisked her cane staff through the air with an astonishing alacrity, given her body weight. Who asked you, she asked, and since no one had asked, we decided not to answer rather than be asked again. We sat in silence. Held our traps. The whole class held its traps. You might say it's not particularly good being a new kid. Everyone is constantly sizing you up, particularly if there are two of you, and even more particularly if the two of you are one. We tried to ease the situation by dressing differently: Frida would wear a richly-laced long white dress with three-quarter sleeves, its lower hem adorned with a cute little red-flower pattern, while I had on a blue and yellow top matched with

 a long, olive-green skirt with white flounces at the hem (sadly, jewelry was not allowed, which always made us feel like we were going out naked). Even so, we were constantly being mistaken for one another. They said it was confusing that we both had the same name, though we thought this should actually make things easier. Not for them, though. Well my little dolls, we were told with unrestrained superiority, the

custom around here is to call two identical copies by different names. So they wouldn't be so identical. There is a certain logic to that, we said when we still thought there was some sense in debating them, but you must admit that another view is equally acceptable: if two identicals are identical, then their names should be identical, too. The multiplicity of such systems of logic is known as "cultural difference." This got a big belly laugh out of the whole class.

The only one who didn't laugh was the Gypsy boy, Sanyi Lakatos. He could empathize; he knew from cultural differences. I'll smash their faces in if you want, he said. We didn't, but thanked him kindly anyway. *Gracias.* We liked Sanyi Lakatos. He could flip a compass over his knuckles like nobody else. He also reminded us of the boys back home. Especially Diego. Diego was half-Indian, while Sanyi Lakatos was completely Indian. One of us always carried a medallion portrait of Diego until it was confiscated by the lady who taught chemistry. She said it was distracting us from the compounds. If she only knew how wrong she was! The best chemistry in the world was the kind we had with Diego, but those washboard-chested toothpicks couldn't even imagine what that was. We were much more developed than they were: for one thing, we already had mustaches, something they found—how should we put it?—*off-putting.* (Alright, they gave us hell for it.) They said that sort of thing wasn't done around here. Said we couldn't be assembling for patrol like that. Said a Pioneer couldn't go around looking like that. Thank God, we

said, one less thing to worry about. Needless to say, we shouldn't have said that. There's no God around here, screamed the homeroom teacher, and her face, glistening with oils, went all red. No she said, just listen to Comrade Lenik and our pal Comrade Principal. (We wondered about this Comrade Lenik, but dared not ask any questions, thinking this would only make matters worse.) Pack yourselves right off

to the principal's office, and take your report cards with you. Our pal Comrade Principal (if he was our pal then we were the mayor of Teotihuacan) received us with excessive smarm, which only made him more frightening. He inquired, and I quote, what had brought us there, and had we perhaps gone a step over the line, and now now girls, let's have a confession before I get all in a huff. Since we didn't know why we were there, we said nothing. Girls, he said, better not squinch your eyebrows like that when talking to me, or things will really get ugly. Unfortunately, we were in no position to satisfy this request spliced into a threat, given that we were stuck that way. It was no use Grandma Kaló's telling us a thousand times, Oh Fridas Fridas, don't squinch your eyebrows because you'll get stuck that way. We just wouldn't listen. We squinched and squinched until, one day, we just got stuck that way. Hence we were in no position to satisfy the request of our comrade the principal, and told him as much. To this, he responded that we would deeply regret this, and sternly asked for our report books. Our comrade the principal got to writing and writing. We envied him this facility; as for us, we could spend all day pondering the right words. There we stood, in the middle of the principal's office, and suddenly became aware that the lazy spot of afternoon sun had faded from the national emblem on the wall, framed by sheaves of wheat. In other words, dusk had fallen. Alright then, said our comrade principal at last, there we are. Now, you two just take this home for your father to sign. And I'd better not see you

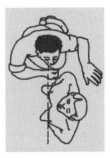

here any more because, well, now now, he said unctuously, which sent a shiver down both our spines. Once out in the half-darkness of the hallway we had a look at what he had written. Read it through twice: "Frida bleated during class in a manner unbecoming a Pioneer. For this I am issuing a principal's warning." Father rolled with laughter at this for three days and nights until finally we had to call the doctor to

bind his diaphragm. The doctor praised us for notifying him in time because, and I quote, one more giggle and *hasta la vista*. At this, Mother had a crying fit and remarked that one of us would have been handful enough, let alone two. But no helping that. There were two of us, said Mother descriptively, and that's that. But what happens, thought we in horror, if one of us dies before the other. On the one hand this would be a rude disproof of our mother's axiom, which wouldn't be such a bad thing. Much more horrible would be being left alone to ourselves. This thought was so unbearable that we determined without delay to do something to prevent this. And so it was: we filched a scalpel and clamp from the doctor's bag, and once he'd left we went into the bathroom and set about connecting our hearts. Our reasoning was that if we could make the two of them one, then

we could not die separately, because the other one would also be me. Our biology teacher would have given us a B+ for this (because, and I quote, an A is only for the most exceptional). Upon completing the procedure we cleaned up the bathroom after ourselves and then, with the satisfaction of a job well done, took out the trash and did the dishes without so much as being asked. Our mother gave an uneasy smile.

As we set off for school the next day, Frida was me and I was Frida. Even though one of us dreamed in Spanish and the other

counted in Hungarian, one liked soccer and the other gymnastics, one sawed wood while the other crocheted, one liked boys (especially Diego) and the other one girls (especially Marlene Dietrich, who also came from abroad and was in the class next door), one was an alto and the other a mezzo (so in chorus we had to negotiate the overlap), but let me say right here that we weren't about to sing

forwardcommunistyouth because that would have given us, as Grandma Kaló used to say, the willies, but instead we sang "The Girl from Ipanema," dum-de-dum, and "Off in the Gumption Fields of Russia," because even if we didn't know what gumption fields were, it sure sounded promising and, finally, though one of us was a Virgo and the other a Libra (this ultimately got sorted out) because we were born right before and after midnight, now we were one, and our heart leapt for joy at how we had cheated fate. But this was just where the trouble began. It turned out that the class picture was scheduled for that day, which we had forgotten all about, what with the heart operation and all. For the class picture you were strictly required to wear the Pioneer outfit, and there we were, not only not in Pioneer outfits, but just the opposite. On top of it all we just then noticed that through Frida's white lace you could see not only her open heart but her breasts, too, which was expressly forbidden by troop regulations. What's more, she couldn't really close off our artery with the clamp, so blood dripped all over her beautiful snow-white dress (which actually went surprisingly well with the color of the pretty little flower pattern on the hem, but still seemed somehow untidy, and undignified for a Pioneer, particularly for the class picture). My blue-and-yellow top was unaffected, but we couldn't work out the heart thing except by pulling it outside of the material, which is

undoubtedly a somewhat unusual procedure (subsequently an article praising it appeared in *Science*), but since this was our first attempt at anything like this we were happy that it worked at all.

There was, however, an aspect that was not exactly such a great solution, either esthetically or practically, in that the artery connecting our two hearts had to be run out the sleeve of our blouses, and it ended up wound around my arm, which really put a crimp in my movements. There's no denying our execution was a little shoddy (though the instructions on the poster said be clean and precise), but we sure would have liked to see who could do better in their bathroom at home. Well, we got an earful. What was going through our heads. Where did we think we were living. Did we think we were in some imperialist bedlam. Did we maybe think the sky was a double bass (this one we didn't understand at all; we'll have to ask about it when we get home). Did someone pull us out of the dump perhaps, or even worse: from the clutches of the imperialist capital—in other words, were we associating with some bad characters.

We did not know the answer to any of these questions, so we just held hands and said not a word. Let go of your hands, this isn't folkdance class. We didn't let go. Well at least get out your Pioneer kerchiefs. We didn't (we weren't carrying them on us, and besides). Do something with yourselves at once, or else. But Miss, we have just now done something with ourselves, and this is it. Then—¡ay,

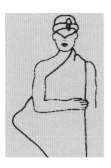

mi corazón!—all inferno broke loose. We shouldn't even think of sitting for the class picture like this. We should not consider ourselves members of the class. In fact, we were class enemies, unworthy of being preserved in memory and even less worthy of serving the homeland steadfastly like it says in the anthem. This had gone on for a solid twenty-five minutes when we decided we weren't going to listen to it any more. We blocked the sound from our ears, the sight from our eyes, shut our teacher and this whole crazy country out from our open hearts, imagining ourselves back at Acapulco Bay, back on the Yucatan Peninsula, back on the pyramids of Tikal, Tulum, Chichen Itza, Copan, and Uxmal, back in the jungle, back in our happy Mayan past and the arms of Diego. Then something unexpected happened: the photographer, silent until then, spoke up. Excuse me, he said softly, if you will allow me an observation, there's no reason, as long as they are here, to exclude them from the event. He was doubtless motivated by the documentary impulse. He doubtless wanted to record the entire truth. He doubtless would have liked to do his job with precision and would have preferred not to be obstructed. Later, his thinking went, everyone could do as they pleased with the pictures: cut them up, retouch them, tear them to bits, burn them or disown them, but as long as he had taken the trouble to bring his equipment, why should he be denied the day as it was, right there before his lens in all its fullness? Why should he be compelled to suffer humiliation in his own eyes, to relinquish his professional pride? Our homeroom teacher glared at him in disbelief. But, comrade photographer, you see how they look, do you not? I see, answered the photographer. You see that they can't just take a seat with their young comrades who are all in ceremonial uniforms, do you not? I see, answered the photographer, but they could be in another picture. Well, comrade photographer can do as he pleases with his own materials, but you can be dead certain that the school won't be paying for that picture. Not a problem, answered the photographer with the calm of a lion trainer, I'll foot the bill for that. He could say that because he was in the private sector. We could only

look on in astonishment at such goodwill and cosmopolitan generosity. Girls, said the photographer turning to us, first I'll take the class picture, then you're next, alright? We were so moved we could only nod. Then we all went out to the courtyard, and when he was done with the commissioned class picture, he waved that we were next. Our homeroom teacher, forbidding all further nonsense, herded the class back into the school building, leaving us on our own to do as we wished. This was not such an ideal day for pictures, the sky being menacingly silver-gray and black: it looked like rain. He motioned us to sit down on the bench where the janitor liked to catch some sun. Take whatever poses we liked; all he cared about was that we look right into the lens. So we sat and took each other's hand, and looked at the camera. Our mother stuck the resulting picture in the family album and wrote next to it, in her tiny little nervous hand, *Frida and Frida, 6th grade, 1969*. Here it is.

We were particularly happy that Diego was in the picture too. *Viva la fotografía. Viva la vida.*

Hand on your heart: Do you always wash your hands before an operation?

What do you conclude from the fact that a frog heart keeps beating even without the frog?

In your opinion, what does this tell us about the frog? Also: Is this healthy?

Physical Education

(tower, dive, forward, backward, inward, reverse, straight, pike, tuck, free position, somersault, twist, armstand, starting position, approach, takeoff, flying action, entry, running re-start, hands joined, toes pointed, arms upraised, degree of difficulty (DD), dives with limit, dives without limit of DD, judge, referee, synchronized diving, protest, drawing of lots, penalty points, failed dive, strong wind, incorrectly announced dive, diving before the signal, losing one's balance, outside the line of flight, side view)

1.

Take your spot and just do the usual. Nothing flashy. Maybe give them a reverse (*renversé*). They usually go for that. A nice clean one. Like you did last year in Sydney. Actually there was a little

puff of wind kicking up there, though the judge never said anything about it. I could have drowned him in a teaspoon. Or right there in the diving pool. Show the whole world how a diving judge who can't even feel the wind (*vent*) can drown in a diving pool. And still I nailed it. Made that little adjustment in my drop (*la trajéctoire*) and by the entry (*pénétration dans l'eau*) I hit the water like a goddess. A female

Poseidon. A Poseidonna. There's a pretty good wind here too (*vent fort*). Well sure, at this height what did you expect. You still have to do it. And impeccably. No second starts, no blemished dives, no protests, no fresh drawing of lots. Just a flawless dive.

2.

Take your spot and just do the usual. Nothing flashy. Maybe give them a corkscrew (*tire-bouchon*). Simple, but looks great. They usu-

ally go for that. Like the one you did in Atlanta. The crowd went wild the first time you dived for the US team. Grateful and enthusiastic. Knew what they were seeing. Appreciated what you were doing for the country. Your new country. *Ask not what your country can do for you, ask what you can do for your country.* Here's what I can do: a perfect corkscrew. It was never perfect enough for the old country. Nothing was ever perfect enough for them. If you won a silver, not to mention bronze, there was really no point in going home. Fine then, so I didn't. The cir-cus fleas can do their jumping for them now. Need to decide whether to do an armstand dive (*plongeon en équilibre*). If there's TV coverage (*course* there is) it comes across better. But maybe not risk it in this wind. Can't lose your balance. Diving off-line would be a fatal error here. No—just take your spot in

starting position (*position de depart*) and do the usual. *This* crowd will go wild too. Home pool. They'll be grateful and enthusiastic. And they'll know what they're seeing.

3.

Take your spot and just do the usual. Or maybe a little something flashy. Maybe give them a somersault (*plongeon périlleux*). They usu-ally go nuts for that one. Though it's true, bouncing on the board (*rebondir sur le tramplin*) usually works out better for you. Not so

much the tower. Or at least not always the first time. I mean, there's a tower here. One-time opportunity. Have to think it through. Can't mull it over too long, of course. Must make a decision. Now. This instant. Still, it would be great if they saw this at home—*they*—if they saw that yes, after all, I can do a somersault from the tower on the first try. The hell with them. That would be my sweetest compensation. They'd see what they've lost. They'd see they lost and I won. Alright now, let's go, maybe no bouncing, but you might work in a run (*l'elan*) somehow. Just have to throw together some kind of approach. Tables, chairs, stuff like that. No, I don't think there's time for that now.

4.

Take your spot and just do the usual. Nothing flashy. Maybe give them an inward (*retourné*). A dolphin dive. A favorite of children and adults alike. The dolphin is the most lovable aquatic mammal. And the most lovable aerial mammal? That'll be me, right now, for a fleeting moment. Queen of the Air. Darling of the air (*chouchou de l'air*). Fifteen minutes of fame compressed into fifteen seconds. Might not even be that much. Who knows, we're pretty high up. But are we high enough for me to create something enduring? What if the camera doesn't catch it right? What if they don't film it at all? What if no one sees the perfect dive? At least you'll have the satisfaction of knowing you created something perfect. You'll know it. That's enough. Now let's go.

5.

Take your spot and just do the usual. You can play it flashy, or just straight and nothing fancy. Maybe give them a pike (*carpée*). Pretty straightforward. The simple things are the most beautiful, and sometimes the hardest to do. Looks easy, but everything has to

come together for a perfect execution. Concentration, balance, the right momentum, and stick to the line. A pike—who never tried one as a kid? Still, there are things, and there are degrees of difficulty (*coefficient de difficulté, CD*). There are things that can only be done one way, but there are others that can be done with different degrees of difficulty, different nuances. You can jump from the sunlit, grassy shore of a

lake, or from a cliff into a rough sea, or off a graceful, arched bridge that was later bombed to dust into a fast-flowing river of inexplicable turquoise, or off a rowboat into a lukewarm lazy backwater, or right out of the starting block into the pool of a health spa basking in the cool mountain air, or off Dad's shoulders into a late-summer lake, or into the thermal pool in the next town over (though the sign says *No jumping!*), or off a sailboat into the waters of an ocean lapping the shores of a south-sea island. You can do it any way you want, except one: you can't dive carelessly or sloppily. Diving must always be precise. Disciplined.

6.

Just take your spot and do it. The usual. No big deal. Throw off a tuck (*groupée*). Nothing jazzy. No gimmicks. You can't fool them into thinking you're really going to wow them with this one. But anyone with a decent eye will know what they are seeing. Appreciate it. Anyone else—well, what's the difference to them anyway? The thrill will be enough for them. Of seeing something they shouldn't

have. Something special. Something out of the ordinary. Something you can only do with parental supervision. Only the initiated will really understand it. *Those who know, understand.* Isn't that always the way it is with everything? And that's how it should be, too. Not everyone has to understand everything. Too much information can drag you down like pebbles in your jacket pockets. You can drown in it. Information sticks in your throat like a fish bone at lunch that pops right out of the gullet back into the open air after a properly-executed Heimlich maneuver. Just a tuck now, nothing more. Take your spot, then take off. Tuck.

7.

Take your spot, then do it. The usual. *Un peu* flashy. You build a trampoline (*tramplin*). There must be a board somewhere in a build-

ing this size. An approach, then a bounce, then throw off a double somersault. The kind that makes them hold their breath. Even the judge will give you a standing ovation. By the way, who's the judge here anyway? I'd like a look at the one I'm supposed to win over. To dazzle. Enchant. The one we're up against. The one running the show. He likes it on the spectacular side (*spectaculaire*), I can see that, but this time he's gone a little too far. (*De trop.*) Like my grandmother Renée said the first time she saw the Empire State Building. Things like that provoke the wrath of the Good Lord (*le bon Dieu*), she said. Things like that are trouble. Things like that bring trouble. She said. Renée was a wise lady. If I had only listened to her more. On the other hand, Renée didn't like diving either. She said it brought trouble too. But you can't always avoid trouble. It just comes. Diving, though, is necessary (*nécessaire*).

8.

Take your spot, et cetera. You'll improvise during the flying action. No—you'll improvise something absolutely *amazing* as you fly. The important thing is to be at the top of the dive list, the only one they show clips of, so the whole world watches your dive again and again, in an endless loop. You'll be the star beyond all question. The megastar. The idol of an entire country: American idol. It won't even

matter any more whether the dive won gold, silver, or bronze. It'll be worth all the money in the world. Everyone will be dying to see it. Night and day, in slow-mo and speedup, in stills, enlargements, in color, in black and white. This dive will have everything. It will be so complex, so intricate, they won't even be able to determine the level of difficulty (*coefficient de difficulté, CD*). They'll be stuck. Oh yes.

9.

Take your spot. Just because. Just so they'll see it. Just so they'll see it can be done like this too. Not to pull your tail in. Not to shrivel up in fear like a California raisin. Not to view it as something horrifying. See the possibilities in it instead. The bounty. The gift, so to speak. Here it is, take it: a gift. At that, you take your bow and give them a faint little smile, and you take it. You accept it—understand? Sometimes you have to accept it. You can't always be kicking against the pricks. Can't say *I didn't ask for this. I don't need it. Take it back where they got it from. Exchange it for something better.* No. You have to take it. To acknowledge what belongs to you. You have to allow that it is yours and no one else's. It's a door that no one else can enter, just you. So enter. Jump.

10.

Just get up. There. And do. Do it. It will contain all of your accumulated knowledge to date. A veritable little capsule of knowledge. A visual knowledge-capsule. They can analyze it for weeks. They'll study every aspect of it—in fact, they'll be teaching the whole thing. You'll be in the curriculum; there'll be exams on you. Kids will be all nervous about it, they'll be saying, *if I can just get through this,* they'll be thinking, *then the rest will be child's play.* They'll love you and hate you. Envy you and idolize you. Anyone who doesn't like you will

still be forced to admit, *I gotta say, that little bitch really nailed it.* And whoever loves you, well they'll be energized just to think they might have become your friend. *Oh yes, I knew her,* they'll be saying, she was open and very nice, always happy, or at least that's how she seemed. Whoever you allowed to get really close could even see what was behind the seeming. *I was close to her,* they'll say, *the closest anyone could get.*

They'll be lying. They'll all be pushing and prodding and elbowing for position and bragging. And lying. They'll be human, flawed. I'll forgive them. Like now, say. In advance (*en avance*).

11.

Just. Because. You have no other choice. This is where every dive you've ever made, everything that's ever happened, has led you. To this big dive. This is the reason for everything. For you to get this one right. Of course the best thing would be a synchronized dive.

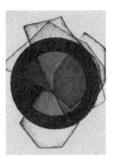

That would be the most spectacular thing. There are two towers after all—but are there two divers? Who knows. Who knows who all is over there on that other tower, and what they have been taught. Whether they know anything that will be of use to them now. We learn so much over the course of our lives, and then, in the final deciding moment, in the finals (*finale*), there is so little of it we can actually use. I am grateful to have been taught, to know how to do something that will be of use to me now. What's more, it is the *only* thing of use to me just now. All my other knowledge, for this brief moment, is useless. Addition, multiplication, rules of the road, names of planets, names of cheeses, what color goes with what, who painted sunflowers, what was Truffaut's first film, who is the father of Sophie's child, what undulant fever is, Pascal's nickname for his mother, the capital of Uganda, and what rivers flow backward. Useless, all of it. Only this. Only this means anything at all. Being able to do a good dive (*savoir faire*). If I could pull off a synchronized dive, then all my wishes would be answered. That would be the ultimate beautiful thing, unforgettable. Who would you want to dive with? (Fundamental question.) Think that over, just hypothetically. Then when you have it, jump. Even as a solo, it will make a big splash. Believe me.

12.

Take your spot and do it. Yes: the usual. Even if the occasion isn't usual. Even if the occasion is highly unusual. Even if the place is unusual. Even if the reason is unusual. Unique. Unrepeatable. Unexplainable. Unbelievable. If it worked from that tower, it'll work from this one too. Try to imagine that you are down there by the diving pool. The diving pool is where you first had to fight for your life. Swim class for children was right there in the children's pool, next to the diving pool. After you learned the basics, they tossed everyone into the diving pool. The children's pool was half a meter deep, but the diving pool was ten meters deep. Whoever couldn't swim got pulled out, but wasn't allowed back in class. Even drowning seemed better than that humiliation. I swam my way out. I could stay. Later it occurred to me that if my first success came here, why should I go anywhere else? So I dived. A lot, and every which way, and better and better. Even the birds only gaped in astonish-

ment. That tower was five stories high, and this one is a hundred and twenty. I'm on the one hundred seventh floor now. If I could do it from there, I can do it from here. From either one all you see is the water anyway. The rest doesn't matter.

13.

Take your spot and do it. Give them a tight little solo. The synchronous diving is history now: the other tower collapsed. Strange,

because they hit this one first, then that one. And still that's the one that went first. The first shall be last: sometimes not so bad. There was really no point in your picking a hypothetical partner, since the hypothetical partner's real tower really fell. Collapsed into itself like someone who has just received tragic, unbearable news, forming a huge pile of glowing embers. Found out it was finished. That's what it couldn't bear; for a while its flame glowed like a shining crimson X-ray in the dazzling blue sky, then it gave in. Sometimes trees do it too, from one moment to the next, they die. Fire blight, they call it. Except that trees die standing up. Let's jump now before it's too late.

14.

Stand on your spot. Just stand. Just standing. And standing. Strong wind. Unusually strong wind. A never-before-seen kind of unmanageably powerful wind. Astoundingly strong wind. Hands together. Teeth clenched. Breath held. Eyes closed.

15.

Just take your spot *and*. There's always an and. Then suddenly no more ands. We always assume there is an and. Experience, too, shows there always is: first one thing, then another, then still another, and over and again. Life is an and.

16.

Just take your spot and blow it. Get too flashy. Lose your balance. Jump the gun. Leave the line of flight. You do a bad dive—no, not a bad dive, but they announce it wrong. They reject the protest. The judge and referee are blind, but only you can see that. Because everyone's blind, they just think they can see. No more announcements or drawing of lots. A nightmare. Thank God it's only a nightmare. Reality

looks better. In reality, it will go well. You'd die if it didn't. If it doesn't go well, you'd rather have drowned in the diving pool when you were four. But it will. Reality always looks better.

17.

Just take your spot and take off. The takeoff (*le départ*)—they say your whole life flashes before your eyes then. My life is a series of takeoffs, one after the other. One on top of the other. So then at the moment of takeoff, I review all my dives and rate them. I try to score my dives objectively. That's the hardest thing to do. Everyone is biased about their dives; there is always some explanation of why it worked out the way it did and not some other way. There's always some cause to explain the effect, the dive. Scoring objectively—that's the hardest thing to do. If there's a judge who scores fairly and profession-ally, that makes things easier since you can just rely on the judge. If you've got a bad judge you can always give them a piece of your mind, argue, lodge a protest. But if there is no judge— just because—then you score yourself, which is the hardest thing to do. Because one always knows how these dives really are. Score them too high or too low, and everyone always knows. And there's no one to argue with. That's the hardest thing, there's no disputing that.

18.

Just jump, then a flying action. Can be watched from the side, from

below, from above, axially, from three-quarter view, circular view, spiral view, square view, or mountain, valley, decline, sun, moon, general, dog, hamster, poppy-seed, honey (even poppy-seed-and-honey, weather permitting), king, *grande dame*, camphor, hashish, history, geography, love, and death views. Then the over-and-over views. That's the good thing about it. Can be viewed in all kinds of views.

19.

Tower.

20.

(Forward, backward, reverse, straight, pike, tuck, free position, somersault, twist, armstand.)

21.

Strong wind (*vent fort*).

22.

Finals (*finale*). Starting position (*la position de départ*). Takeoff (*le départ*).

23.

Flying action (*la trajectoire*), hands together (*les mains réunies*), toes pointed (*les orteils pointés*), entry (*pénétration*).

24.

Scoring (*résultat*).

Complete the following sentences:
Look before . . .
One swallow doesn't . . .
One small step for a man . . .
My God, My God, why hast Thou . . .

Homeland /
Environmental Sciences

Fidelio
(a blog opera)

Wednesday

They made me an informant. Day before yesterday, on the internet. That's the fashion nowadays. My handler's cover name is Don Fernando; mine Jaquino. They've been after me for at least two years, but this time they're blackmailing me with something they were sure I couldn't shake, unlike the previous occasions. They said they'd fill the media with the news that I wasn't, as it were, "purebred." Mother would not be able to deal with this. (Besides all the other consequences, I can't handle camping at all.) Plus they would air out all my, and I quote, rutting tendencies. They told me to report on everything happening within the walls of the Institute. Marcellina has a new hairdo (this doesn't interest them at all, but it does me), she is beautiful as ever, but this time it's truly heartbreaking. She couldn't care less about me. Nothing new there. *Well, we'll see.*

Friday

The Institute is a fascinating place. Never a dull moment with Don Pizarro, as we shall call the boss. Last night for example, when

everyone but me was sleeping and the lights of the boulevard (World Heritage Site) flimmered drowsily through the window, Don Pizarro's people smuggled someone in, supposedly an investigative journalist. People say he intended to shop incriminating photos to magazines showing Don Pizarro wearing, for example, the brassiere with its Arrow Cross Party emblem that he wore under his bulletproof vest. This would not have been particularly advantageous for him right before the leadership elections, not to mention his party. The hooded guy was unwilling to fork over the negatives, for which he was threatened with starvation and torture until it killed him and not a soul would know where he was. He seemed like a pretty tough kid, refusing to disclose how he managed to take the pictures. Personally, I have an idea but I shall keep it to myself. This might come in handy later. I named the journalist Florestan.

Sunday

Through his moles in the press, Don Pizarro spread the word that Florestan had been captured and executed by the opposition. He even made a bogus video about it, a very clever piece really, though the editing job was pretty rough around the edges. Naturally it was argued this only demonstrated its authenticity, though in my opinion they just hadn't the faintest idea how to fake it right. You can crank out ideology about anything of course, but the truth is I hate shoddy work. When I start something, I intend to do it right. Even my report writing is getting better. Not that I love it, exactly, but as long as you're doing it, do it properly: editing, style, register, focus, what have you. It's just another profession. If Marcellina found out what I'm doing, she'd probably despise me. I wouldn't really mind. At least hatred

has some feeling to it. Her apathy is driving me crazy. Even dogs get treated better. I have to figure out something to sweeten her up on me a little. But oh, what? What?

Wednesday

So I've come up with a diabolical plan. It's so devious I can hardly follow it myself. But it will work. It *must* work. As I see it, there's no other way. I found out that Florestan has a gorgeous wife—let's call her Leonora—who is going insane with grief at home since he disappeared. I got a message to her (I have my ways), informing her that her twinkly-eyed husband was locked up here, adding what she had to do to get into the Institute. As there has been an opening ever since the assistant to Marcellina's old man Rocco got bumped off by the members of the city council (no doubt hired by Rocco and his brothers), I told her to apply for the job—under a cover name, natu-rally—and, as for fake papers (ID card, diploma, lan-guage exam certification, etc.), I told her to feel free to turn to Wallenberg, Inc., who produce outstand-ing quality work (i.e., protection against the moronic gendarmes) and not even one of the Russkies would catch her out. And she shouldn't worry that she was a woman, I said, because the last National Council meeting voted for a women's quota, and seeing that the Institute was pretty crappy in that department, they'd just have to take her on.

Monday

If only I could win the lottery this easily. Alas, I am a genius, even though no one gives a rat's ass about me. Especially this Marcel-lina woman. But now we'll just see if I can bend the story (and her wasplike waist) to my whims. Naturally, I'm keeping schtum about my own doings in the reports; I mean, things haven't gotten to the point where I will turn myself in. (Though who knows, maybe this will happen someday after all since, as Don Fernando likes to say in his fits of melancholy, inscrutable are the ways of state security. I am inexplicably starting to like Don Fernando. There's something soothing  about him. He has become the pivotal element in my life. He counts on me and makes me feel human, even indispensable. He respects me. Who else treats me like that?) As for trivial developments, I report on them faithfully every single day. These include the fact that once Leonora had immediately set to work, Rocco took her around the Institute and explained its operations to her. One of these, for example, was to supervise the work of the Bone Brigade. This was a 17-member team that manufactured plastic skeletons for the GDR. Or at least on paper that's what they did, but as soon as the Croatians and Iraqis became the biggest customers, the whole thing got a little suspicious. I told Leonora to get to the bottom of this when she had the chance, so I could write it up and warm Don Fernando's heart when he saw that his trust in me was not misplaced. We're starting to be a little like father and son. Recently he praised me so highly for my loyalty that, he said, he was going to call me Fidelio from now on. Nice name. (Nicer than Fido anyway, however you look at it.)

Tuesday

My plan worked out. I knew Marcellina wouldn't be able to resist Leonora's exceptional beauty and charm. Naturally, I had also known beforehand which way the wind was blowing in her case. After all, I'd had plenty of time and inclination to watch her, and actually I probably knew what would happen even before she did. Unfortunately this did not diminish the passion I felt for her; on the contrary. Whatever the case, Marcellina fell deeply and hopelessly in love with Leonora who, poor thing, tried to be nice to her to avoid angering Rocco and thereby blow her cover. As it happens, she was always trying to get away from Marcellina, who was on her like a bloodsucking leech. Now it was time for that little bitch to find  out what it's like to be consumed by passion when the other person couldn't care less about you. This was my sweet little revenge. When Marcellina learns the truth about who Leonora really is, she'll need a shoulder to cry on, and there I'll be, right at hand, lending a kind ear and even consoling her a little, if it comes to that. I'll be nice. Friendly. Indispensable.

Thursday

 The regrettable events of February are coming at a crazy pace. It came out that the Great Leader was preparing to make a personal visit to the Institute, which would involve a whole PR hullabaloo. This sent Don Pizarro into a panic that Florestan's kidnapping and torture would come to light and be trumpeted all over the international press, and it would be curtains for our accession to the EU, not to mention his own poor little head. He ordered Rocco to dispose of all incriminating traces that very day. In other words, knock the journalist off. The response from Rocco, who had accumulated his share of professional pride, was that he would be willing to torture or beat him, and even be kind to him if absolutely necessary, but he refused to do any killing, as this was not in his job description. He punctuated this with a stamp of his little hobnailed boots. Don Pizarro rolled his eyes at this, in anger as much as in despair, and in a little

snit about how he had to do everything around here, he left it to Rocco to dig a grave in the backyard of the Institute and do something, at least, to earn his paycheck, and hop to it. At this, Rocco—already in fear of being let go and transferred to the Ministry of Education as Chief Executive of higher education reform—grabbed a shovel and scuttled out of there in a hurry. But then Leonora, having heard this whole little heart-to-heart and now terrified to death for her precious Florestan, badgered the old man until he allowed her to pitch in. Rocco was glad not to have to dig an unmarked grave all alone, what with his back acting up, not to mention having hands and feet all tied together with the "ruomatism" that had been torturing his fingers for the last month. Yes, that's what he said: "ruomatism."

Thursday

My wireless connection was out this afternoon, so I'm only just now getting back to this. Once Rocco and Leonora had managed, through tremendous exertions, to dig the grave, they pulled Florestan out of his cell. He wasn't exactly in top form, believe me, scarcely in condition to stand on his feet from being starved, to say nothing of the treatment he'd gotten from Rocco. Seeing him Leonora sobbed her 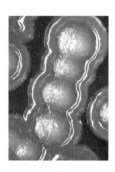 eyes out, which sent her costly Revlon eye shadow rolling down her cheeks. Right behind her, naturally, was my Marcellina, who similarly burst into tears to see them embrace, sending her own costly Estée Lauder eye shadow rolling down her cheeks. And behind them, of course, was me, observing the scene with satisfaction, without sweating so much as a drop since I use Old Spice Deodorant, which offers 24-hour protection. The mood was such that we could easily have cranked out a nice little quintet. Then Don Pizarro dashed in, telling us to make ourselves scarce because he didn't like being watched while he worked. But I saw Leonora slip behind a column, and once Don Pizarro had run through a few painful goodbye tortures, which he just *had* to record with his new digital camera because he loves taking pictures, he pulled out his heater to finish off Flores- 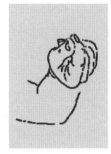 tan, and then Leonora suddenly jumped out and, shielding her man with her body, started waving a little pistol with a mother-of-pearl handle right in front of Don Pizarro's nose. They were about to put on a simultaneous endgame when one of the minions ran in to say Don Pizarro should make his way immediately to the reception desk because the Great Leader and his posse had arrived. Well, it sure looked like Don Pizarro's rage would send his psychosis into relapse. At that point, though, no one knew what was coming.

Thursday

I lost my connection again, though time is really pressing for me to write my report. While Leonora and Florestan were nibbling at each other, Marcellina, having witnessed the whole show from behind the other column, burst into hysterics and, after reciting the entire periodic table, began frothing at the mouth and fainted right  into my arms. Then came another gofer and said everyone should assemble on the Appelplatz because the Great Leader had announced a general amnesty before the accession to the EU, and wanted all the prisoners to muster up for him. I'd sure love to see that, I thought, and I have to write a report anyway, so I left Marcellina on a recamier with a compress on her head and followed them out. There was a surprise in store. One of the journalists in the Great Leader's entourage recognized Florestan at once, and the whole mess was cleared up. Don Pizarro was led away in handcuffs while his rights were read to him. He was screaming that they'd see, he'd be turning to the court in The Hague, at which everyone had a good chortle to see that there was still someone around who believed such a thing existed. Then the Great Leader said Leonora, for her brave action, would be awarded a Knight of the Cross medal with the image of Tereshkova on the March 15th national holiday, and also informed the crowd that Leonora and Florestan were actually his long-lost twins, meaning they could not be man and wife, but at this point what difference did it make. Then there was a general hoo-ha where the folksy types spanked their bootlegs in jubilation and the city types did a low-key break dance, and the bourgeois meticulously vomited out the red carpet while the traitors to the fatherland

soused vodka in the pantry with the Russians. As for the Gypsies, well, finally everything was in order with them. All's well that ends well, I thought, because at that moment Marcellina appeared, a little pale and unsteady, looked at me with those melancholy eyes of hers and said, "You are my sole consolation. Come, let's go for a walk."

Friday

I finished my report. Don Fernando will probably be satisfied with me. What a shame we only stay in touch on the internet because I'd love to get to know him more. Of course that would put the kibosh on my cover name. After all, there's no doubt that the best thing about the internet is that no one knows you're a dog.

P.S.: Am I naïve? Woof.

WRITE AN ESSAY on the topic of "My Summer at Camp!" Pay close attention to the juicy parts!

WRITE AN ESSAY entitled "My Big Brother, the Melancholy Kapo"! Be objective!

The Foundations
of Our Worldview

The Goblin

The smell of wet overcoats and the slopping of winter boots in the mud on the black-and-white cobblestones. An uneasy impatient hubbub in the room; interminable lines despondently snaking toward the service windows. The people crammed into the main post office clutch Christmas cards, letters, and packages of various sizes and shapes as if these were their sole hope of redemption. The minute hand of the large round clock on the wall ticks forward laboriously, as if every movement causes it pain, each station of its progress marked by a loud clunk. Every eye stares holes into the shoulders of mildewed overcoats smelling of naphthalene, or is fixed on the sluggish clock. The owners of dreary, rain-soaked furs, sodden camelhair, swollen wadding, and cockily strutting men in foul-weather gear wait around for the moment of final unburdening and, thus released, of return-

ing to their lives, to the grungy, clawing air redolent of winter, to time freed from its pothole, starting up again. Colorful knitted caps, bonnets, gray-brown hats, fur Huszar busbies, tasseled shoulder wraps, billed caps winterized with earflaps, and headscarves all undulating in the steamy hall like marker buoys in some foggy northern sea. Somewhere amid it all is the teacher, Mrs. Fuchs (Aranka to you), lost in thought, her cloth jacket now worn to glossy in its seventh year. Where is the holiday in all this? What can be the point of all this suffering?

The holiday, begins Aranka haltingly to help pass the time, stands apart, embodies a *différance*. But based on what? Just a red letter on the calendar? *As the lightning, that lighteneth out of the one part* under heaven, shineth unto the other *part* under heaven? An unexpected event? The flash of a smile; an inbound night tram? Is a holiday like dry clothes after the storm perhaps? Buttered bread with green peppers on a summer afternoon? A fuma-  role tucked into the snowy mountains of Transylva- nia—is that what a holiday is? An autumn lakeshore in the sun? A velvety hillside? If so, then how did I end up here, muses Aranka Fuchs resentfully. What am I doing in this cranny of space-time, this dark, woeful cave, this force field in which walking is just barely possible? No; the holiday must be something

 else, supposes Aranka, at which the clock on the wall clunks ahead in relief. Even a correct hypothesis drives time forward. At this, Aranka takes another stab. The holiday might be a new beginning, a con- structive reset to zero, the gift of a fresh possibility, a marker of one age passing and another beginning. Ebb and flow: the holiday is the border motif of our time, the background music for existence. Hence, Aranka opines, life without the holiday is a sound- lessly running silent film, a tense and pregnant silence. A shabby fox stole is panting on the neck of the preceptor Fuchs. Perchance the holiday is the warmth of a pigsty? An inhalation? A hazy steam, a body-on-body? But then what of the soul? For the holiday—is it not so?—is made of the soul as well! She runs a plump hand over the reddish lock of hair clinging to her forehead. In the sparsely lit hall, the distant service windows glimmer like tiny campfires in a snowy night landscape. These are the longed-for destination of the

crowd wearily shuffling toward them, those beckon-
ing, flickering, warm beacons, the promised light
marking an end to their agonies, their struggles: the
moment of redemption.

Well then the holiday is an arrival, an event, a
happening; an occurrence that we may count on—or
not—thinks Aranka Fuchs, stringing a pearl neck-
lace of diffusely glowing thoughts. So that would
make it a dramatic plot, a dramaturgically polished, gleaming stone.
This puts us in the theater, reasons Aranka, a thought that fills her
heart with warmth, as there are few things in life she loves as much
as the theater. Indeed, all the world's a stage, she adds cleverly, and
we await the entrance of our protagonist, for the grand *entrée*. She
gives a barely perceptible nod of the head as if in approval. So then,
our task is to attend, to focus—a thought that decidedly gladdens
Aranka since she has always proven gifted at both. This, then, is
the holiday's message: to live with an open heart and open eyes, and
we will certainly know, when it comes, what must surely come. But
if this were all there is to the holiday, she continues respectably (for
Mrs. Fuchs, the teacher, is no midwife to facile conclusions), then
what is the point of these snaking queues, to what end this committed determination? There must be something more here, some
missing component, a link in the chain, that ties it all together.

Then she is struck by a realization, causing her some shame not
to have thought of it sooner. Well of course! Why else would all of
these sodden, coatwrapped people be standing here if not to make

contact with others, presumably their loved ones.
What could be the point of a package except to
give a signal, a signal of ourselves and of our love,
that we are thinking of them, that *a thought has been
given*. So then the holiday is both communion and
communication, proclaims Aranka triumphantly,
at which the big hand of the clock wearily clunks
once more. The wheel of time turns steadily but

carefully. But this being the case, adds Aranka, her face now aglow, we should spread the word, be prepared to converse at every moment, with everyone, ready to extend an arm to a stranger, welcome their presence, and accept what they have to offer us. You must know how to send and to receive—this is what contact is, and what is more, it is the ideal form of touching. And the most beautiful metaphor for all this, the crowning symbol, its *locus classicus*, is the post office. Once Aranka Fuchs reaches this point in her thoughts, her soul fills with tranquility, now colonized by a profound peace. Because if this is the case, then she now finds herself, on the eve of the holiday, in the best and most magnificent place of all. At this, Aranka is freed of all concern for the spotty lighting, the steamy mildewed air, the odor of naphthalene, the gray puddles at her feet, her soaked shoes, and even the raggedy fox stole breathing on her from behind. She was happy to have the privilege of spending the eve of the holiday in the best of all possible places. She wouldn't even mind if she had to stand in that snaking line scrutinizing the lights of those distant service windows until daybreak the next morning.

Now Fuchs's attention is caught by a stir of movement that breaks the curdling of the stagnant afternoon. The mound of wadding immediately in front of her, which until now had stood motionless, suddenly comes to life when a tiny old hunchbacked lady emerges from it, unpredictably turns and stares right between Aranka Fuchs's eyes with penetrating, close-set, blue eyes of her own. Aranka, hitherto convinced that the long-awaited moment of communion and communication had arrived, looks back encouragingly at her with an innocuous smile. At this, the old lady opens her mouth to gibber a pronouncement: "This will not be a good Christmas," a sentence that pierces Aranka's heart like an ice pick. Bewildered as to whether she has really heard what she heard or whether her imagination is playing some

sort of cruel trick on her, she asks, with a stutter, "Are you speaking to me?" (Though that brief thought clearly was directed at her, of this there could be no doubt.) "Yes, you," responds the old lady with some impatience, as if conversing with a mental defective. This twists a strand of icy fear around the heart of Fuchs, while a tornado of everything that might give credence to the old lady's words blusters through her head. Her fears now acquire shape; her previously repressed anxiety is palpable. Aranka's heart thuds ever more

fiercely, her stomach a spasm of constriction, while she searches desperately for a handhold, a loophole, an escape route. Her mouth dries up, her tongue sticks to her palate. She wants to speak, but no words are forthcoming. Not a sound can she muster. Then, after several tries, a few clears of her throat, she somehow ekes out a few faltering words: "But . . . but . . . how do you *know*??" Aranka Fuchs has

some hope left yet. Now maybe she's got her, and this freshly stirring ragpile will be compelled to admit that she has no idea. That she is nothing but an evil spirit that can vaporize from the face of the earth at the slightest breeze, never to return. With her razor-thin mouth, the lady gives a disdainful smile like one who sees through sophistry. Again she looks Aranka right between the eyes and, after a beat, says "You'll see."

With this, she turns to face forward, reverting to a mound of rags in the murky, grimy hall.

The clock's minute hand acknowledges this with a tick. The pregnant hour turns on.

The postal worker is regarded as a folk hero in the United States. WRITE your opinion on the perceived status of the Hungarian postal worker!

WRITE AN ESSAY on your favorite holiday with the title "Why I love Christmas"!

Geography / Biology

The Temptation
of Henri Mouhot

In the jungle Henri sweats and pants. He's fat, and scant of breath. A bug man is not supposed to be fat. A naturalist is not supposed to be fat. A heroic Lothario is not supposed to be fat. An explorer is not supposed to be fat. A language teacher in Russia—now *he* can be fat. Those ten lousy years with those lousy brats had ruined him, Henri thinks, slapping at mosquitoes in his rage. Damn little blood-sucking vipers. Mosquitoes, brats—in the jungle, Henri's stream of consciousness flows freely. Henri says lousy a lot. His wife hates him for that. But here, in the jungle, he says whatever he wants. Thank the Lord for animals and plants, thinks Henri, a fierce Lutheran, who nevertheless gets on swimmingly with Catholic missionaries, although. Along with lousy, Henri's favorite word to say is although.

Henri has reservations. Henri is tortured by reservations. Is it any good for us to be here? Or more precisely, who is it good for? Or to put it in a more refined way, what in tarnation are we doing here, *parbleu*! Henri frequently says tarnation and *parbleu*, for which his wife hates him. But here, in the jungle, he says whatever he wants. Henri has a British wife, while he himself is French. [Is this a problem? Argue

pro or con!] Anna, the great explorer, is the daughter of Mungo Park. It will come in handy to be explorers, thought Henri back in the day, before he had discovered anything. Henri, the future son-in-law of the great explorer, thus quickly discovered networking. But this is not why we like him. We like Henri for his gifted pen, *le style c'est l'homme*, and for his long red beard. His wife has asked him more than once to shave it off. Beads of sweat drip from his long beard straight into the jungle. The Lao are crazy about Henri's beard. They cry out in excitement whenever they see it, and groups of children follow him wherever he goes. The children bring Henri rare bugs, for which he reciprocates with copper wire and cigarettes. Then the children let go of their mothers' breasts and puff like old opium addicts. Henri says this is the accepted way around here and we shouldn't

worry about it. And anyway: it's bugs above all else. Henri kids not when it comes to bugs. Not long ago, for example, he lost an entire collection chock full of rare specimens that sank in the harbor at Singapore, but Henri didn't let this eat at him and began a new one forthwith.

No, Henri did not let this eat at him. What eats at Henri is the inexplicable certainty that he will croak here, right here in the Laotian jungle. Henri has a dark foreboding. Henri should not be here at all, thinks Henri. Henri should be shuffling off out of here

because his forebodings have all been accurate so far. Like when he boded fore that Anna, daughter of the illustrious Mungo Park, was cheating on him with the druggist, that miserable Bovary, back home in Jersey. And then, as was bound to happen, he caught them going at it one afternoon in the back room at the pharmacy, where he had initially gone for bugscotching chloroform, but as things turned out he needed smelling salts more, not so much for himself as for Anna, who had fainted when catching sight of Henri as he looked into the back to complain when no one had come out to the counter, because that day Emma, the druggist's wife, had gone into town for her big weekly shopping, or at least that's what she said, but Henri had his usual side-door foreboding about that too. In the steamy jungle Henri's beard quivers at this unusually vivid flashback. In flagrante, *parbleu!* Better the jungle, the bugs, the leopards, the rhinoceroses, crocodiles, scorpions, centipedes, leeches, and pythons than the white-hot blinding rage from seeing that sanctimonious horse-faced, horse-toothed, vinegary wife of his, that horrid little wheezing *anglaise*, being squashed by this dickhead Bovary. It's not as if he cared that much, but still, the concept of *honneur*—well, even a sweaty, rapidly balding, fiery-bearded entomologist prone to weight gain knows about that, and not just from the dramas of Racine either. No. Henri might have

been well read, but he was no dummy. He immediately recognized what he must do. He packed up, and before you could say Jack Robinson he had already discovered Angkor, which instantly made him an ever-fixed star or, as we would say today, a pop star, by which point he had forgotten all about that scene at the druggist's when news reached him, deep in the jungle, that Emma in her shame and despair had poisoned herself with one of Bovary's concoctions,

but still Henri got no satisfaction from this because he was actually fond of Emma, a splendor to behold with those green eyes of hers, or whatever color they were—much more fond of her than that horse-faced tart—and pitied her, poor woman, since it was clear she was bored to tears in that druggist's day after day and was dreaming of an utterly—*utterly*—different life. All the same, Henri writes not a word about this in his diaries, well of course not, he thought, why get everyone's juices flowing when he himself was already pushing up the daisies. Let us focus on flora and fauna.

The fear eating at his soul like vultures on carrion came from the foreboding (Anna would call it a *presentiment* with a typical pucker of her lower lip, which always made Henri think *précieuse ridicule*, but where he read that he could not recall) that there, in the jungles of Laos, somewhere near the confluence of the Mekong and the Nam Khan, he would meet his end. He will then be 35. Thirty-five, quick calculation in his head, would make it 1861. If you really think about it, that would be the same number as the current year, ponders Henri, really thinking about it. *You are my destiny*, Anna would be singing, as surprisingly resonant tones emerged from her surprisingly flat chest, but where she got this tune—in this heat, well, no, he had no idea. No use, declared Nietzsche who knows where, it's not yet cold

enough to think. But then what am I doing here, thinks Henri, a little stunned by his own stupidity. *Que sais-je*, was the phrase that flashed through his mind, free-associating there in the jungle, no fucking clue. Ke-sayzh, ke-sayzh, he murmured rhythmically to himself, a rhythm that provided the pace for his eradication of what, in his professional capacity, he called fascinating Southeast Asian flora, but privately just rotten vegetables. For this there is no explanation. Legion are the secrets of the great. "Phrai," says Henri to his faithful Thai servant, "has a woman ever betrayed you?" Phrai gives Henri a contented smile, as is his wont. "No worry," says Phrai, as he does to everything, whatever the subject. But Henri's fierce Lutheran soul couldn't give a rat's ass about Buddhism. Henri's fierce Lutheran soul would nail Anna to the doors of the Wittenberg Castle Church.

Each of her fingers separately, each with its own tiny little nail. Henri would remove them from between his teeth, hammer them precisely into her pale flesh, just as he mounts beetles on cardboard. Anna as a large, swart-backed, disgusting coleopteron. Here in the steamy jungle, Henri sweats, his red beard quivers. With his machete he takes great slashes at the thick, liana-like vines. A halved snake lands on the  tip of his dusty boot. Henri glowers indignantly at his prey. He has a foreboding: dammit, now this. But onward now, ever onward, beyond the jungle of the Fire King to parts whence the travel guides say no white man has ever returned. Of course, what kind of idiot would swallow what travel guides say, thinks Henri, and spits to remember their awful style. They not only lie, but *en plus*, offend common taste. Nail them all up to the Wittenberg doors, fumes Henri's

Lutheran soul. "The hell with them," Henri says out loud, at which Phrai nods in approval. "No worry." Let's get on then, thinks Henri, to Luang Prabang, where King Tiantha is expecting me! At this joyful thought he takes a swig of Calvados, though in his diary he writes that all he drank was tea that day. "I too know how to lie, my dears."

King Tiantha, indeed, was on pins and needles. For days now he had been agonized by a mysterious premonition of a visit from a red-haired, shaggy, flabby giant whom he must welcome, with full pageantry, that his people and land might survive. But said giant must not sense the king's fear, lest he fly into a rage and mow everybody down with his machete (by Gillette). All the same, once Henri had arrived in the capital precisely nine months later, they made him wait around for ten days so he wouldn't think they were thrilled to bits about his being there. King Tiantha could hardly contain

himself in his excitement; he had no idea how he would manage to get through those ten days. When, finally, Henri was led before him, King Tiantha was stretched out lazily on a couch, apparently ignoring his guest. He lay there, languidly, his heart pounding, slapping at flies. In those parts he was known as the Dissimulator King. "Hey man, what you doing here?" asked King Tiantha, but Henri was at a loss how to answer this unexpected question. After all (as Anna would say pretentiously, *that is the question*), what on

earth was he doing here, where no white man had ever set foot? Was it not his purpose, as an agent of boundless human greed, to heap more troubles upon these already imperiled people? But the two men quickly became fast friends, and before you could say Jack Robinson such a fairy-tale banquet was assembled that the next day everyone was laid out flat, to the accompaniment of general heaving.

As the poetess writes, great communal spewings put the seal on friendships. Henri and King Tiantha became such fast friends that, in time, they came to regret it themselves. Fortunately no one saw them. Henri would gladly have lived a carefree life at Tiantha's court in Luang Prabang ("just like Geneva," writes Henri in his diary, "only shockingly different"), but one fine day Tiantha informed him that, not so far away, where the Mekong flows into the Nam Khan, lives the Great Stinkbug which, King Tiantha told Henri, who was now sucking his thumb in wonder, no one had ever caught, and whoever saw it could never forget. Once Henri had removed his thumb from his mouth, he proclaimed "If I don't catch the Great Stinkbug, then my name is not Henri Alexandre Mouhot!" (Notice that in saying this, he actually didn't say anything at all.) So with a heavy heart he packed up his things and took his leave of King Tiantha and his court, and set out to catch the Great Stinkbug, the dream of every entomologist and nightmare of every layperson. Here

Henri was seized by a feeling (*The horror! The horror!* As Anna would say with her usual nerve-racking yammer): corner of Mekong and Nam Khan, check, 1861, check, and since everything seemed to be in order, he set off so as to arrive in time. And not to waste *your* time, I will fast-forward and tell you that, while he didn't catch the Great Stinkbug, at least he caught a good case of malaria, and turned thirty-five on the very day that, enfeebled by fever, he scratched his last words into his diary: ". . . have mercy on me, O Lord . . ." To which he added—just in his head—the following: "Anna, you worthless tart, someday you'll cry for me and I won't be there."

---

1) Is this a problem? ARGUE pro or con.

2) DO YOU LET someone who says they are exterminating bugs into the apartment?

Military Education

A Box of Photos
(captions on the back)

Jolika in a hat. Why is this so important to have? An apprentice milliner in her first hat? Who cares? Why should I get all mushy about it? Just because it's sitting sassily cockeyed on her head? Just because her black curls peek out so lustrously? Just because she's got such a mischievous expression that the camera trembled in my hand? Is that why the image is a little fuzzy? An ill-timed movement? But who moved: me, or her? Which of us took the first step toward the other?

Jolika with her mother. When she smiles, Jolika's chin takes on a little point, just like her Mama's. I should have chased Jolika off that very second when she first aimed that pointy little chin of hers at me in the hat store like some deadly weapon. Thank you miss, I don't want a hat. But still, what was it you had in mind, Sir? Nothing at all. Least of all hats. If there's anything I've thought of in my life, it was a pointy-chinned, saucy little apprentice hatmaker. Saucy but sad-eyed. Easy to love. Who sees with those sad eyes how easy it is to love me, too. Laughs at my jokes. Doesn't mind that I'm fat. Wants pointy-chinned children with me. I really should have chased Jolika off.

Jolika in Esztergom at the Mária Valéria Bridge. We crossed it and visited Grandpa, who lived with the Slovaks. The sun was out. It was nice with the Slovaks. I spoke Slovak myself; we had a nanny *bei uns. Nye kritch, nye bodaj, alle budye ridg bozaj.* Not supposed to shout because she'd kick me in the ass. Or the pussy. But I was just a little boy, *nye* pussy on me. What about now—what am I now? And what do I have? Well, the photos for one. *Do pitchu.*

Jolika in Herkulesbad. If it's good enough for Franz Josef and his Lizzy, it's good enough for us, was my thinking. *Ausgetippelt* suited for a honeymoon: Scanning the map, I determined the place was at the intersection of 45'52"North and 23'52"East which, delightfully, put it right in line with Venice. So a trip to Herkulesbad is a symbolic trip to Venice as well. I like symbolism and coincidences. Here in the Cerna Valley are to be found the most beautiful baths in Europe, said Franz Josef. And as it happens, here in the Cerna Valley is found the continent's most beautiful Jolika. So said I. The photo is an allusion to my opinion. Performifies it, you might say. And now—now what does it performify? Thanks to the prevailing western and southwestern breezes, the average temperature in Herkulesbad is 10.5° C. You could bite the air. You could bite Jolika. I should also mention the presence of *pinus nigra* on the lonely mountaintops (What the Lumberyard Manager Saw), as well as the very widespread appearance of *syringa vulgaris*, in other words the common lilac. But no lilac is ever common. Neither is Jolika common, ever. But I will tell you that, in this place, I was a veritable Hercules.

Jolika in the foyer at the Opera. My mother always said *fo-ah-yé*, as if in wonderment. Jolika is wearing my mother's mink stole. A fine little mink stole that I sent to the Red Cross last year so the homeless could keep warm in the cold. Mother never said *homeless*, because in those days there were no homeless, just the "Land of Three Million Beggars" (an operetta). The land of three million beggars did not attend the opera, though the foyer was always nice and warm. Too warm for me. Me, I like the cold, those crunchy snowy winter nights. Jolika handled the warm foyer just fine, even in her stole. Jolika could handle any-

thing, never complained. She only complained one single time, that you couldn't put the yellow star on your stole because, I mean, how would that look? Jolika had a sense of style, just what a milliner needs. I wanted to be a conductor, but for the time being I was a lumberyard manager. Which is why we would go to the opera—so I could observe the conductor. Jolika loved the drama, and the fo-ah-ye. *La Bohème.* Where's my muff, where's my little gloves. Things like that.

Jolika with her little brother Ernő. Ernő was a wretched little boy, like the time he sliced up Jolika's new hat model with a hedge cutter he'd filched from the gardener at the zoo. Still, little Ernő was a sensitive child and didn't like losing. If he was found at hide-and-seek, he'd throw a fit. If he lost at high-risk poker he would drink himself under the table. If he fell behind the other swimmers, he would turn around, head home, and rip his swimsuit to shreds. Little Ernő would do anything not to lose. Just couldn't take it. Like in '38, when he got on a ship and didn't get off till he reached Australia. So much did he hate to lose that he felt doomed when others would have been hard at play and loving it. Jolika and little Ernő were inseparable. Ernő begged Jolika to go to Australia with him. To which Jolika responded: What—now, when the shop is doing so well? What about Mama? And Dezső? (That was me.) And what about the season tickets to the opera that we've already bought? Little Ernő

threw a fit. He knew he was going to lose. Next day, he got on the train to Lisbon. On the third day, the hat shop was shut down. And we couldn't go to the opera anymore. That one really hurt.

Jolika is packing. She's packing my rucksack because she was a supremely gifted packer, indeed a veritable packing virtuoso. I made no effort to take over for her, so obvious was her supremacy. As I was in great demand, Jolika was constantly packing, and she impressed every time. Jolika never had to do a test pack like other earthly mortals. She had only to look at something to size it up, register how big it was or what would fit in it. This came in handy for hatmaking, too: what kind of head fit into which hats, what kind of hat was a match for which heads. Things like that. The boys were always amazed. Who did your packing so carefully that they even got that field shovel in there? Proudly I would show off my suitcase to everyone. Naturally there were some who didn't get all that worked up about the efficient use of space; they were more interested in the sausage and cigarettes. You always get a few lunkheads. They don't know art when they see it. Not even interested. Why are they even alive?

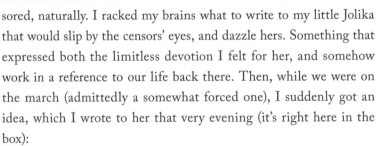

Jolika is reading a letter. My letter (who took this picture?). Normally only postcards were permitted, but once a month we could write a letter too. Censored, naturally. I racked my brains what to write to my little Jolika that would slip by the censors' eyes, and dazzle hers. Something that expressed both the limitless devotion I felt for her, and somehow work in a reference to our life back there. Then, while we were on the march (admittedly a somewhat forced one), I suddenly got an idea, which I wrote to her that very evening (it's right here in the box):

I'm amusing myself looking at all the headgear, stretching as far as the

eye can see. Gray hats, beige hats—mostly beige, all the rage these past couple of years. A few of the old gentlemen have been wearing those very narrow-brimmed hats you usually see on young fellows, but there are some black ones too, surprising to see on these hot October days. There are also some caps around that the golfers and tourists like to wear; even their clothing is sporty. O these lovely cloth caps, travel caps. I used to be a little monkey like that once, bought one of those travel caps in my youth to wear on a trip abroad. But there are many other kinds here before me, the inexpensive kind worn by so-called little people, shopkeepers, factory hands, workers, market hawkers—even panhandling peasants are wearing them these days. [section smudged] If they ever take a hat census, there would be more people in the world wearing caps than hats. I kiss your hands. D.

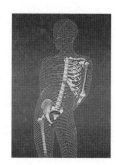

I was hoping she'd take the hint and, in addition to the hats she was secretly creating, start making caps, because they were obviously moving better. As for the slightly fusty people-smell (as mother would call it), I thought it best to remain silent. Why get my Jolika all worked up. Then there are the censors to think about, of course. Writing is such an involved undertaking. Music—well, that's my world.

Jolika on Pozsonyi Boulevard, in front of the door to our building.

Over the doorway, as decoration, is a star. Looks quite good up there. Jolika looks at the camera, laughing, waving (at me) with one hand and holding her belly with the other. Or not holding, really, but rather gently touching, unconsciously checking that it's still there. The skirt of her ensemble clings to her proudly. It's made of fine English material for which I'd traded some firewood. As Mama used to say approvingly: "Oh that Dezső is such a clever boy." Mama liked pretty things too. But Jolika looked damn fine even in the simplest things. Not to mention when she got dressed up, like this time. There is only one thing that spoils the whole image. She's laughing, but her eyes betray her.

Jolika on the bank of the Danube (newspaper clipping). Jolika loved the Danube. Sometimes we would swim across it to visit Grandpa  over with the Slovaks. I sure wasn't a bad swimmer— I played water polo for the Esztergom Sport Club, after all—but Jolika could dart like an otter, passing me underwater in a blur, then call out to me, teasing me, with a laugh, to try to catch her. On summer days, the water droplets sprinkled over Jolika's raven locks would sparkle in the sun. At the very latest, I would catch up to her on the shore, and grab her, and we would end up rolling breathless on the ground. Grandpa would have a snack of latkes waiting for us. Jolika standing on the near edge of a long row of people on the quay with her jacket, shopping net, and shoes next to her on the ground like everyone else. The net was full; she'd been shopping. I know those shoes well, bought them for her in Vienna on Kärntner Strasse. They were chestnut-brown with Goiserer stitching, with suede uppers and leather soles. When she first tried them on, Jolika raved that they make a great leg, even though she had no need of a shoe to make her legs great. Jolika used to say you could tell a gentlewoman by her hat, her gloves, and her shoes. The *accessoire* is what makes it all, Jolika would say; everything else is incidental.  Not a bit surprising, this philosophy, coming from a milliner. Jolika standing gracefully in her stockings, with one hand resting unconsciously, gently on her belly. Strangely, she is looking straight at the camera as if having caught sight of the cameraman taking potshots. She looks upward, sideways from the line, with the Margaret Bridge in the background.  Although her face is serious and withdrawn, there is a mischievous twinkle in her eyes, like someone who has run through a number of thoughts and arrived at a resolution. I know what she's up to. Jolika is about to jump. She will jump, then swim, darting around underwater like an otter. She will leave everyone else behind. Finally she will surface around Csepel, and swim on to the Iron Gates of the Danube and on to the Black Sea. The water droplets sprinkled over Jolika's raven locks sparkle in the sun.

This is what I was thinking when I bought the paper and saw the photo.

One is constantly thinking all sorts of things. Then not thinking them.

Burn them. Burn them all.

IF IT TAKES ONE SECOND for you to hit five targets without reloading and you don't get interrupted, then what time in the afternoon does the water change color?

DO YOU EVER secretly play with Daddy's gun? Do you always check that the safety is on?

Religion

We sat on the seashore in distant Borneo. We sat and sat, then out of nowhere we spotted a text in the water. (Impatient, we smashed the bottle to bits on the rocks.) This is what we read:

We often trysted in the night zoo, hoping not to be so conspicuous. There was a day zoo as well, but the pitiless sun would have been a problem, aiming vertically down on us to reveal our most secret thoughts. We were half a degree from the equator and ten thousand degrees from freedom. Besides, the heat was a bit less stifling at night. Cool was nowhere to be found, only barely distinguishable levels of heat. Sometimes, after a tropical downpour (which usually hit us like an unexpectedly powerful orgasm that was just as quickly over), the sun would drink up the moisture from the steaming asphalt. Two minutes later, even the very memory of rain had vanished once the diligently maintained sewers had swallowed up the implausible volume of precipitation. Normally I would get on the bus at the Bras Basah Road stop, right on the way to the zoo. It ran all night, almost empty of passengers. I lost myself in a Malaysian soap opera on the bus video screen, all the way to the end of the line. The night zoo was the last stop. I have no idea who came up with the idea of starting a night zoo, but he was clearly no run-of-the-mill intellect. Still, like any brilliant idea, this one was surprisingly simple. You don't have to be a scientist or biologist to know that animals, particularly the wild ones, are generally most active at night. In contrast to day zoos, where we see the inhabitants lazing about here and there in the sweltering heat, their muscles clearly unwilling to make the slightest twitch except at feeding time, life in the night zoo is teeming with spellbinding activity, full of comings and goings, of

contact, eating, lovemaking, bathing, and looking in on the neighbors. Living their lives, in short. What is more, the well-conceived and refined illumination only heightened the spectacle; you might even say it put the whole undertaking in a good light. The lamps were tucked in between the branches of bushes and trees so as to be gentle on the eyes of the animals, not to frighten them. Even the brightness and color were adjusted to create an ideal setting. Sometimes all you could see was the animals' silhouettes against the background of the steaming, blue-black night, like figures in the shadow plays that are quite the popular genre in these parts. As for the visitors, they felt as if in some sort of mystical, undecipherable dream from which they hardly wished to awaken. The more docile animals were allowed to walk around on the path with us. The tapir, for example, liked to plop right down on the tracks in front of the little zoo train like some despairing heroic lover, but after a little prodding and encouragement, was convinced to abandon his original plan and sniff up the amblers with his outsized, perceptive proboscis.

My heart began to pound even at the entrance. We hadn't seen one another for a week, and missing you had become almost impossible to bear. At times we managed to rendezvous more frequently. Often the weather would have a say, since if the sky was falling there wasn't much hope for an outdoor meeting.

All other locations were out, given our situation and because both of us were being watched. Naturally, apart from the weather, there were other factors influencing the frequency of our meetings. We had to be careful not to attract the attention of the authorities with too-frequent encounters. In this country, our love was forbidden, a crime calling for a punishment from which recovery was not so inciden-

tal. Corporal punishment was allowed, even idealized. In their ideology, depriving one of freedom of movement was senseless without adding physical punishment. Hence the number of years in a sentence was accompanied by the same prescribed number of hits with the cane, driven into the furrows created by previous blows. Their thinking was that feelings of guilt, just like feelings of love, were only really absorbed by the flesh. I can attest that your touch was not only absorbed by the flesh, but burned in brand-like. At that point there was no driving it out. It was indelible, leaving a lifelong mark

whose surgical excision would have reduced me to nothing, like a vanished thought. My body, my soul, indeed my entire life had meaning only through you, could exist only through you, reached fulfillment only through you. The unit by which time was measured was the agonizing period between our reunions, all else was measured by this, everything acquired meaning in relation to it. Stepping through the entrance gate, I felt my cells come alive, my pores

open, my senses now working with unnatural sharpness and precision, as if under the influence of drugs. I took in your scent from a distance, long before catching sight of you. I felt, I knew, that you were nearby, which was enough for my sense of smell to fill in, not just the time passed since our last meeting, but even the remaining space stretched taut between us, enough for me to take in the fragrance of your body. Most of all I liked to sniff behind your ears, in the hollow of your neck. What I found there—well, I thought it

would be nothing for me then to snap the neck of a feral cat, to claw its living flesh into strips, to summit a twenty-thousand-foot mountain and lick off its snowcap slowly, at leisure, letting the flakes dissolve over my tongue. That scent makes me feel I have finally come home, the place I am always meant to be, the secret inner realm, and from there I can move onward, inward ever more, to the very depths of velvet darkness, the place of no return, with no reason to return since nothing exists but this, or whatever might exist is nothing but an empty husk. The gift of your smell is the promise of a future, igniting the traces of your touch on my skin like a magic wand, bursting into flame, one after another, like a thousand tiny light bulbs strung over a baobab tree at a festival. A shudder ran along my skin like an electric circuit; I could distinguish every touch in my mind, each with its own location, its moment in time, its name, and I saw your face, too, accompanying them as they ignited one by one. Ah yes, this one was on the shore of the Indian Ocean at dusk in the lukewarm sand, when your flashing white teeth bit that scorpion-shaped tattoo into the thin flesh above my breast; this one was when we escaped the torrential rain ducking into the covered garden of a prayer house, pressing our backs into a stone wall hewn to its ultimate inch, where the entire company of gods bore witness to us drinking, licking, sucking the manna out of each other to the very last drop, like hungry jackal pups, then again and again until the storm subsided. Then once we had lost our way in the woods and could no longer see the markings on the trees, and there was nothing to make out to the end of sight and all we had left was to mark each other's unfolding skin and flesh to help us find our way back to the world because leaning there against the tree trunk we had become one with the molecules of the air, absorbed into the pores of the ferns, sinking into the moss, and as we wriggled in the traps of flesh-eating

plants we figured we might as well just surrender and become dark-purple colorings on its petals, the color of your bite marks; then when we looked down on the village from the grassy hillside there were great comings and goings in preparation for some celebration, and while the festive food simmered in huge vats, some were tanning animal skins, thrashing them with cudgels of bamboo, all to the beating of drums, and then we decided to celebrate with them in our own way, letting the holy day unfold in all its glory, memorialized

forever, and the arc of our backs was a perfect fit in the arc of the hillside, and whichever of us happened to be on top in the embrace without end, without aim, had her back warmed by the sun, since fulfillment was not focused on one sole point but instead, like a tenaciously extended note at a piano matinee, unexpected and irreproducible, where the sleepy audience that wanted nothing more than a post-luncheon nap was wholly irrelevant, and where each successive note made their unprepared hearts ever more uneasy, unlike the evening big-name concerts where even at the coatroom they knew they were in for an enchanted evening of wrenched hearts and tight throats, and so were not caught unawares when that is what they actually got, no, in fact they were anticipating it, expecting, desiring it, and once they had it they all nodded in satisfaction, yes, that's what we were expecting and now we can go home, but

here, listening to an unknown musician with the languorous afternoon sun slanting through the concert hall windows to glow lazily on the far wall, highlighting some details of the gilded plaster statues and stuccoes while plunging others into shadow, and out of nowhere comes an unexpected melody for which we had steeled ourselves even less, then suddenly you get the feeling as of a sharp tool plunged into your defenseless heart and, as if that were not enough, it persists there in the skin and flesh of your chest and bones, unresponsive to attempts at removal, and indeed penetrates deeper the more you try to wrench it out, and finally we come to accept it as something that will remain, being now where it belongs, and we entrust ourselves to it, perch on it ever so delicately, letting it carry us wherever it would go, like out of this concert hall into the afternoon sun, even out of the city and up a sunlit, grassy, distant hilltop where a tenaciously extended note leads us on into the night, into the next morning and the countless successive unbounded epochs, and yes, as the funeral procession led by a swan carriage passes by to bury the old village priest, a coach for the deceased, adorned with colorful carved wooden swans, pushed in silence by the villagers in their colorful headdress, a few of them standing on top, by the casket, to ensure it does not slide off, and at the very front of it all, in the position of honor, stands the oldest man in the village, who looks to be 120, trembling as he holds fast to the coffin with bony, liver-spotted hands so as not to also slide off into the great unknown—and at this point we stepped forward from the wall and took our place in the procession,

following them to the edge of the jungle, where a great pyre stood on a spot freshly cleared of undergrowth, and atop it an enormous wooden bull whose hinder parts gaped open to reveal a hollow; through this opening they pushed the coffin into the bull, following which the villagers put in the mementos, devotional objects, and gifts. All went inside the bull, and once the line finally ended and every mourner had placed his sendoffs by the dead man, quiet gamelan music could be heard from beyond the clearing, from a place deeper in the jungle, and they ceremoniously set fire to the pyre, the bull and its contents ignited, smoke rose up, ever higher, to the jungle's canopy, and then I began, slowly and gently, to push into you, or rather just slide in as there was no need for pushing, as if the surging wetness between your legs had been preparing for it, and it flowed all over my hand, my arm, and I just went deeper and deeper, encountering no resistance, and I thought sooner or later I would certainly hit something that blocked me from going further, but I was wrong, things were different, and once it wasn't just my hand, arm, shoulder, head, torso, and pussy, but also both my legs and feet that were inside you, then I found myself swimming, and felt I had found my way back to the original, primordial element, felt that now finally I had found the secret passage, and knew that, if my breath held out, with luck I could swim through the tangle of labyrinths to surface on the other side, up into the sunlight, the air, the far bank

where no one could reach me, where the laws of this place no longer hold, where I am free and forever yours.

I tread the zoo's main allée slowly, with reserve, since running or dashing would have called attention to myself, though I did run through these thoughts in my mind, past the haptic memories of each one in turn, the free-ranging inhabitants of the zoo passing me by: the bobbing gait of the nine-banded armadillo, the collared peccary, two smaller coatis and then a tapir off the mini-train tracks, now roused from his ultimate despair and once again full of life, the pied fawns, long-tailed crowned guenons and, from the rehabilitation center, mischievous orphaned baby gorillas, droop-nosed proboscis monkeys, waddling dim-witted pandas, jaunty mountain goats, razorbacks, duckbill platypuses, kangaroos, badgers, jerboas—everyone who found it necessary to contribute something on this evening to the secret act that would soon take place between us, who thought by their presence to assure us of their sympathies and solidarity, their concern, their love. The larger wild beasts, kept separate by ravines and furrows and gorges of various dimensions, paced excitedly up and down, sensing, even from a distance, the tension in the air, the nighttime lighting dramatically revealing their nervously shivering shapes. The sultry, steamy night was filled with yelps and whinnies and squawks to the accompaniment of cicadas chirring.

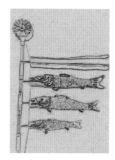

My heart, joining this cavalcade of sound, began to beat louder, more heavily, as I approached the elephants' rock garden where we had our encounters. Now only one solitary turn, elegantly landscaped into the path and lined with rare orchids, was all that separated me from the sight of you. I was certain that you as always would certainly be there first. No matter how I dashed and sliced my way through the city to meet you as quickly as I could, you were always there before me, waiting so calmly, deliberately, as if that were your purpose in life, like someone for whom there could be no more crucial and meaningful activity, as if this one invested all your other actions with real substance. And so it was. For both of us. Now as I took the turn in the path, the air caught in my lungs, my bronchi, and even though I wanted to see—wanted nothing more than to see—for a moment I closed my eyes so as not to see right away what I so wanted, or not to see right away that what I wanted to see was perhaps not there. While my eyes were closed, a bat flapping its wings whipped up a breath of air that surged over the skin of my face. Finally, my pupils, wide open in the dark, took in the sight of you like an overdue promise. There you stood in all your stunning reality, fanning yourself with graceful and dignified movements, but otherwise seeming so fresh and youthful and tranquil as if this were your most natural state. I saw your rose-colored tongue glide delicately over the rim of your mouth, your giveaway of erupting joy. We stood barely ten paces from one another, from a fulfillment that cascades like lava. A powerful quiver ran through my entire body and I felt unable to cover the remaining distance. Finally, once one of my legs seemed willing to execute the command to step and I started toward you, I suddenly felt a hand clamp down onto my shoulder. *You're coming with us*, a voice said. I was immediately spun around and dragged off. I turned my head before reaching the orchid-lined bend. Your sad elephant-eyes followed me away.

In distant Borneo, there we sat on the seashore. We sat and read. Occasionally we mentioned Zion. Then it occurred to us: *Your day of flowering will come, for God loves you as He may, and those who now subdue you shall come to rue the day.*

CALCULATE how many angels can fit on the head of a pin if each angel is approximately 45mm and faithless.

English /
Home Economics

Mrs. Longfellow Burns

(a biography)

[. . .] Henry Wadsworth Longfellow, with his golden hair, his golden hair,
tall and of a port in air, with azure eyes,
in tawny gloves, he took dominion everywhere.

Henry, the national poet, writes verse like a bird sings. From Henry, the national poet, rhyme flows like the trots—oh Mother of God, here's another one—splat! It hits Henry hard that people think just anyone can write poems. Him, for example. *Tell me not in mournful numbers, / Life is but an empty dream! / For the soul is dead that slumbers, / And things are not what they seem.* So it goes. Well, yes. Henry, the national poet, is making culture before the nation has even invented it. "Well, well," says America, "Henry, what is this?" It turns it this way and that, examines the sparkling object, yet still does not understand. "That?" says Henry with his winning smile, "That is the flowering of New England, do you see it not?" In the background nod the members of the New England team, the Patriots: Nathaniel nods, Ralph Waldo nods, Henry David nods, Oliver nods, Herman nods. (The girls do not nod; today the girls are convalescing and have been excused.) Henry sings to himself and plays the flute like some mythological creature. Henry never goes anywhere without his flute. Henry, the national poet, even flutes his way across Europe, stopping at every charming little inn, rustic little hut, and crumbling little bungalow, conversing with peasants,

artisans, and traders, with the silver flute—a passport to friendship—right there in his pocket. Henry at a bullfight in Spain. Henry
in Italy, in front of the Coliseum. Henry in Germany, on the Alex-
anderplatz. Henry in England at a soccer game. He's a fine-looking
boy, is Henry, easy to photograph. A ray of hope warms the heart of
America, the stumbling babe: it shall have its culture, its photogenic
betrothed, its fine-looking bards, its ballsy sages. At 22, Henry was
a university professor, a professor at 22, ha-ho. The hearts of his lady

students beat wildly for him—oh, pardon, he has no
girl students, as they are excused. *Lives of great men
all remind us / We can make our lives sublime / And,
departing, leave behind us / Footsteps in the sand of time.*
(Video clip here: "Footsteps in the Sand of Time,"
Henry singing).

 The first Longfellow arrives in America in the
bleak winter of 1676 from Yorkshire, England. *For
he's a jolly good Longfellow, that nobody can deny.*
Henry's pedigree is pristine. His grandfather had been a general in
the War of Independence, his father a lawyer. Henry was a young
gentleman from a fine house, America's incorrigible sweetheart. He
loves his neighbors and baseball. In his free time, he is optimism
personified. *Not enjoyment and not sorrow, / Is our destin'd end or way;
/ But to act, that each to-morrow, / Find us farther than today.* Onward,
and with dispatch. Henry Wadsworth Longfellow, son of Stephen
Longfellow and Zilpah Wadsworth Longfellow, is born on February
27, 1807, a gray and inhospitable day, in Portland, Maine. Portland is
a harbor, and those born there have a more profound
understanding of the world than the inhabitants of
other, more backwater New England towns. Nothing obstructs his view. The waves may be crashing
and the cold going to the bone and people blowing
into their hands, but the view is great. Buena vista.
Whales and shipwrecks and what have you. Fresh air
you can practically take a bite out of. The fascinating

people buzzing around the harbor, and the buzz of fascinating people stir the interest of the young fellow toward experiences beyond his own, resulting in Henry's attending school at three (see *child abuse*). At six, Henry's teacher writes the following on Henry's report card: "Master Henry Longfellow is one of the finest pupils in our school. His reading and writing are excellent. Furthermore, he can also add and

multiply. His behavior in the last quarter has been exemplary and agreeable." Signed, Mrs. Helen. A gentleman is a gentleman, even in elementary school. This is elementary. None of that "whined all through class" or "shot spitballs at his schoolmates" or "tried to poke out the eye of his deskmate with a compass," or "tugged at the girls' ponytails." (The girls—the girls were absent, the girls were excused, the girls that day, as always, were convalescing. *Oh, sweet sweet girls of the harbor.*)

At bedtime, Henry's mother Zilpah (yes, there really is such a

name), would read to him and his siblings of Ossian, the legendary Gallic hero. This always gave rise to a miniature rebellion, as the children aspired to become Ossian rather than sleep—even the girls, though that would actually be impossible. Then Zilpah would have a hard time restoring order, and always regretted reading Ossian, the legendary Gallic hero, aloud to them when she clearly knew this would incite a rebellion, but there was nothing for it, as the children's hour was sacrosanct, and this is what they demanded, while their Papa was unavailable at the moment. "Every reader has a first book," Henry would later write, as the poet of the nation. "In other words there is one book among all that first takes hold of his imagination, that simultaneously excites and satisfies the desires of his mind." [Can you guess what book this was for Henry? (Hint: his father Dr. Stephen Longfellow used to give him a good thrashing for it with his belt, although, as Henry recalls with a big grin, it was

still worth it, because without this, he would probably have had no idea how to father a child. *See* also:
the role of know-how in American culture.)]

Time moved on, and the nineteen-year-old Henry
found himself a senior at Bowdoin College when
that institution decided to establish a Department of
Modern Languages. But at the committee meeting,
a stick-in-the-mud elder colleague pointed out that,
alas, no one at that institution spoke modern languages. Therefore,
after some consultation, they decided to ask Henry to be the department's first professor, but before that, they would send him off to
Europe for a little polishing up. Henry agreed under the condition
that, in return, they destroy his file, from which it might later come
to light that he regularly reported on his classmates. In the blossom-
ing May of 1826, the flaxen-maned young man set out to see the
world with those sparkling azure eyes of his, and meanwhile make
himself a scholar and professor. As above: flute playing, etc. In the
bleak winter of 1829 Henry returns to his uncultured
homeland where, ha-ho, he embarks upon his beautiful career. But there was something else: the day
after his return, in church, he spotted Mary Storer
Potter, who back in the day had attended the girls'
class of the same year (when not convalescing, that
is) as a fairly homely, freckled, pigtailed, shovel-
toothed little girl, but by this time she had developed
into such a breathtaking beauty (I mean *really*) that

Henry could, as one might logically expect, hardly catch his breath.
His feet were rooted to the spot, and (oh, Lord!) they almost had to
call an ambulance. The voice of the nightingale of the nation caught
in his throat for the first (and last) time. He silently accompanied the
girl home and, in the shivery winter of 1831, took her to wife. Time,
the great organizer, moved on.

In the foggy autumn of 1834, Henry wins the prize for Most
Handsome Professor of the Year, ending up on the cover of *Life*

magazine. For this, he receives an appointment at Harvard, but first he is sent off to Europe again for a little more polishing up, as far as humanly possible. *In the world's broad field of battle, / In the bivouac of Life, / Be not like dumb, driven cattle! / Be a hero in the strife!* Henry takes with him the lovely Mary, who, after a miscarriage, dies a hasty death on the trip. *Mary, Mary, quite contrary!* Henry, *in the bivouac of Life*, decides not to cut short his voyage, bound as he is by the New Deal he had made with Harvard, as well as his gentleman's

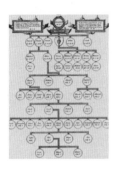

agreement. Even before his return he makes the acquaintance of Fanny Appleton, a wealthy Boston heiress, Fanny (Be Tender with my Love) who will later (time moves on—*much* later) become his second wife. There's no denying that Fanny at first (i.e., for years) had no desire to reciprocate Henry's feelings, as she thought him a conceited, puffed-up windbag, and besides, Henry vexed her to no end in 1839 when he dribbled out the circumstances of their meeting in his prose romance *Hyperion*, which the entire East Coast had set to devouring. Still, they were married unexpectedly in 1843 (*Fanny, what were you thinking?*) and from that point on, their life became a vexing idyll. The couple had set up an outrageously elegant home, provoking the ire even of the normally unctuous Emerson, who lived in considerable comfort himself: "If Socrates were here, we could go & talk with him; but Longfellow we cannot go & talk with; there is a palace, & servants, & a row of bottles of different colored wines, & wine glasses, & fine coats," writes the seething Ralph Waldo.

With his tumbling hair, tawny gloves, and trademark flowery waistcoats, Henry becomes a well-known and romantic fixture of Cambridge life. Girls and ladies all sighed in unison at the sight of him, while the gentlemen tipped their hats respectfully and the youths of the town swarmed constantly about his house to play with his children—five in number, two boys and three girls, *grave Alice and laughing*

Allegra and Edith with golden hair. In the insufferably beautiful spring of 1854, Henry has had it up to here with teaching and the interminable department meetings he personally directed. He resigns from Harvard and invents freelance poetry, which Fanny (alas!) cannot get too worked up about. Furthermore, in the same period Henry begins to meet up with an Ojibway tribal leader and to write a bit about Indians which is, let's face it, a fairly suspicious development. Fanny does not see that this was a national culture in the making, does not see that Old Shatterhand and leather chaps will someday come of this; all she sees is that her husband is never home for dinner because he's down at the old corner public house (i.e., speakeasy) again drinking whiskey with his chubby tribal chief. Time moves on: his *oeuvre* accumulates nicely while the family reserves dwindle. I will allow that there are many things Fanny does not see, but she certainly *does* see that you can't make a living off of poetry.

After the publication of *Hiawatha*, Henry's Indian best-seller, his entire income from poetry in the glorious years of 1855 and 1856 amounts to $3400 and $7400, plus touring gigs, but otherwise his average annual income barely tops the meager pay he had received at Harvard ($1500). Fanny has to scrimp and scrape to put together money for food, as well as for the two pairs of new tawny gloves and fresh flowery vest they purchase for Henry each month.

Time, the great equalizer, moves on and in 1861 Fanny, known to the public as Mrs. Longfellow, realizes one fine day that her food

money has dwindled to nothing, and it was only the middle of the month. Poor Mrs. Longfellow sinks into sorrow, all the while thinking how she might save tomorrow. She must do this by the following day, since if Henry realizes the food money has run out, he will get all worked up and his verse-milk will dry up, and then it won't just be a matter of the children going hungry (*grave Alice and laughing Allegra,*

116

etc.), but to top it all off she, Mrs. Longfellow, will go down in history as the one who threw a wrench into the development of a national culture, which, let's face it, is a bit much. A solution must be found. Meanwhile, the girls, *grave Alice and laughing Allegra and Edith with golden hair,* are upstairs playing with the dollhouse they got from their Papa, when they come over all hungry and run down to the kitchen to make themselves peanut butter and jelly sandwiches à l'américaine. There they encounter their mother slouched over the kitchen table, despondent of her miserable situation. At the children's arrival, Mrs. Longfellow raises her sorrowful Anglo-Saxon horseface to see the wheat-gold waves of her little girls' hair, at which her mind fills with illumination. Not far from the Longfellow home is a Jewish wig-maker, whose workshop Mrs. Longfellow passes nearly every day. In the shop window is a sign: *I buy hair for good money.* These words thrum in Mrs. Longfellow's head like bees in an upset hive. *For good money.* No time to waste in thought; a minute's hesitation will scuttle her plans. "Edith, Allegra, Alice, come here, my little ones!" cries Mrs. Longfellow in a trembling voice, extracting the large, tonsorial scissors from the bureau drawer. Now the hour of the children has truly arrived. *The Children's Hour.*

After the girls have dashed, shrieking and tearful, from the house, Mrs. Longfellow carefully assembles their flaxen locks and folds them into three identical little packages. She prepares to seal the simple brown wrapping paper with wax, as is her wont. But as she heats the wax, it abruptly sparks such a great flame that the packages catch fire, as do Mrs. Longfellow's hair and clothing. Mrs. Longfellow supposes this to be the Lord's punishment. Having accepted the will of the aforementioned individual she does nothing to extinguish the fire, allowing the flames gently, unhurriedly to lick at her all around. Several hours later, when Henry arrives home, he finds a sizeable pile of ashes still aglow in the middle of the carbonized kitchen. Henry digs around a bit with the poker to determine the nature of the kitchen apocalypse that has left these remains. He finds, at the bottom of the pile, a sooty lock of blond hair and, on the kitchen table, a letter addressed to him in Mrs. Longfellow's hand. "Henry my dear, forgive me, but I have quite burned through all my cash. The blame is all mine; please do not scold the girls. F."

Here Henry Wadsworth Longfellow thinks: First the Civil War, now this. To soothe his rattled nerves, he sets to translating Dante's Divine Comedy into English. His work proceeds quite swiftly. Years later, Queen Victoria will grant him a private audience. It is unknown what words were exchanged between them, but those who stood at the door thought they heard the words *G-spot* and *unmentionables*.

ANALYZE the following expressions:

"Ars longa, vita brevis."

"A pain in the ars."

Drawing / Art history

A memory: Victorine lies on the couch, staring. *Really* staring. Staring is what this little woman is really good at. That sweetie. Honeypie. That Victorine Meurent, or Meurend, or Meurand, you never know with one of these exactly what her name is, but who am I to talk, people are constantly getting me confused with that scoundrel Monet. (Why doesn't he change his name already, or just vanish from the face of the earth?) She can stare like nobody else. That is why I'm painting her, you see, and not someone else. But the way she's staring today, well, it's more than I can bear. She's staring straight through my skin, this Victorine. Right through to my bosom (can I say "to my bosom"? French is such an odd language). Anyway, it looks to me like Victorine is preoccupied today. What can her problem be? I got her a lovely red flower to put in her electrifyingly red hair, got her a bracelet, got her a stunningly gorgeous, flowery embroidered silk shawl to drape over that sweet little alabaster body of hers that gets me in a sweat just looking at it, got her some soft velvet slippers, and, to top it off, got her the Negro servant girl that she asked for—just to test my endless patience of course, but I did it to prove to her that there's nothing that this insufferable little creature couldn't ask of me, so long as she doesn't leave me for another, which

I couldn't handle either personally or artistically—and then she got a stunning bouquet, and even, at Charlie Bodler's recommendation, an ebony cat whose ebony tail stands permanently straight up (and really, who could blame it?)—all this just to make Victorine happy, but nothing is good enough for her and she's always peevish about it, always something irking her, she always just stares at me with those penetrating eyes but really, I beseech you, is it even possible to paint someone who never does what I say? I've been entreating her

since noon, to no avail, to try just a teensy bit to pose like Venus, just for my sake, assuming she (execrable little munchkin that she is) has any idea what that is to begin with, though recently she came out saying she's a painter too, and just wait and see, the Salon will accept her stuff when they toss me out again. Well, at that I couldn't hold back a smile, which naturally got her irked and she threw the paint box at me, which in turn ruined my quality suit of English material, and at this there's no denying I gave her a good smack because even my gallantry has its limits, even though all the others say I'm a *véritable* limp dick since I haven't even screwed Victorine yet, though I won't say it hasn't crossed my mind at least nine hundred and three times, which is more or less how many times she has appeared before me, starting right with the very first time I saw her last year, to my downfall. At this point this Victorine has been nothing but an albatross around my neck, and I swear if she were anyone else I would have long ago finished nine more pictures too, so this

is all a serious impediment to the development of my *oeuvre*, not to mention that she gets me into the most vulgar and embarrassing scandals—me, who wants nothing more than a respectable bourgeois existence. My mother, godchild to the Crown Prince of Sweden, has declared on several occasions that this humiliation will be the end of me, and it's lucky my father, a judge, didn't have to live through the

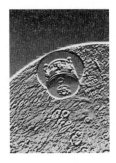

awful scandal elicited by my recent painting. Naturally, Victorine (who else?) was the cause of that too. Because, well, what happened? We went out into the country to do the *Breakfast*, I being happy to be finally out in the fresh air, and to think what a fine little picture I would whip up there, one this lousy Salon would have to take because it would be so far beyond reproach that I'd even scoop up the Napoleon Prize for it, and good old Géne Delecroix's dear little goateed jaw would just drop in astonishment. We'd had everything thoroughly planned, set up the poses, adjusted the clothing, placed the picnic props, and all that remained was to wait for the right light when, out of the blue, Victorine says "Tell me it's not true what I heard." And what might that be, my one-and-only sweet Victorine, jewel of models, who holds my heart in thrall? "That you're going off to Holland next week to marry that dough-faced, cow-assed milkmaid, Suzi, who you said not long ago that you had almost nothing to do with, and that I shouldn't be making a scene because I was the golden ray in your life, who rends your heart to smithereens, and that if you just so much as look at me you lose all control, and told me to just wait and see, I'd be the eternal passion of your life, that I'm worse than absinthe because at least that's something you *can* get enough of, for a while at least, but not me, no. Furthermore, tell me it's also not true when people say that scrawny little midget Léon-Éduard,

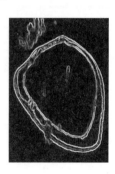

whom you had the gall to claim was the milkmaid's little brother and only your godson, is actually your own bastard child, your little freak of nature, and this lard-caboosed woman wouldn't stop pestering you and now you're slinking off with her to adopt that little disgrace of yours!" The two male models naturally cackled lasciviously, hardly suspecting the tremendous fun that awaited them, and all I wanted was to join them and reestablish my masculine dominance and employer's authority, when Victorine, again, looked at me with those eyes of hers, just as she is doing at this moment, and the blood in my veins ran cold. Her gaze was so threatening, so bitter, and at once so contemptuous that I was at a loss what to do, all the more so since even though she—Victorine, that is—had so utterly subdued my heart, yet her every word was true. But at this point how can I make her believe me? How to explain that Suzi is an earlier, hasty misstep of

mine for which I must, as behooves a gentleman, now take responsibility. Slowly I arose from the grass, dusted off my trousers, and cleared my throat to say "Look . . ." At this, Victorine, in a veritable scream: "Don't say it! Say it isn't true, because otherwise I won't be accountable for my actions!" Well now, if I cannot be a *chevalier sans reproche*, at least let me be one *sans peur*, am I right? Particularly once the truth has been so ruthlessly told. I had no choice but to confess. At this, Victorine sprung up from the grass like one of the Furies and ripped every last shred of clothing off her body while shout-

ing so loud that the whole park echoed "Alright you miserable wretch, come on, paint me. Now we've got your goddam light!" Indeed, the sun at that very moment shone through the leaves at exactly the same angle of slant and precisely the intensity we had been awaiting all that time. It was a perfect, almost otherworldly illumination. I gave one last feeble attempt: "Don't do this, Victorine . . ." But she just screamed back "'Twas not I, 'twas thou, O Édouard!"

At which she just plopped back down on the grass, still in the altogether, right between the two dumb-founded men. Meanwhile, as I say, that improbably silken, providential, early afternoon light poured down upon us, and after all that self-restraint I had been exercising only out of respect for Victorine, this was more than I could resist. I began to paint. The two fellows could hardly believe their luck, though

there really wasn't much they could do, given the strange setting, so they conversed with one another while sneaking embarrassed, side-long peeks. I painted all day long like there was no tomorrow, and believe you me, my feelings were stirred so high that I wasn't entirely sure there would be one.

I finished the picture that same night, and the next day dashed down to the Salon with it. Naturally they tossed me out on my rear, but at least I could hang it across the street at the Rejects.

Then I packed my bags and really did sneak off with my dough-faced Suzi to the Netherlands, to marry her in the presence of her parents and against my better instincts. I didn't even get a chance to tell my mother, godchild to the Swedish Crown Prince, given that she has been lying in a darkened room with a migraine since the scandal erupted, unwilling to admit me.

After our return my days and nights became a blur. I felt that my artistic career was finished if I could no longer paint Victorine. I also felt that if I could no longer see her, then my life, too, would be finished. Finally, I felt that the biggest mistake of my life was not

remaining in Rio de Janeiro in '48, when my juris-prudential father sent me off on a training ship to make a man of me. Since that time, I might have become owner of coffee plantations all over the country, with fifteen Negro servant girls attentive to my every wish, and, above all, I wouldn't give two shits about painting. Wouldn't even know what it was. My God, why do you never offer guidance to your imperfect son, why do you always leave him to his own devices, why?! Long story short, I went off to implore Victorine. I implored her by day, implored her by night, spent nights with the dogs on the threshold at her door, where we bayed at the moon together. I promised everything she wanted, just as long as she let me paint her again. After two months, three weeks, two days, thirteen hours, and twenty-seven minutes, she ultimately relented, but with conditions. She told me I could paint her, but only as she wanted it. Do I need to mention what a colossal blow to my artistic integrity this repre-

sented? Still, I was willing to do anything as long as she would model for me, as long as I might again regard her alabaster skin, her crimson mane, her soft lashes, her adorable freckles. Opium of my life, do with me what you will! At that, my one and only Victorine pronounced the following: "You may only work in my studio (her "studio"!), so the sessions will take place exclusively there, and you must acquire the following props: one golden bracelet, one black chok-

er, one silken kerchief embroidered with flowers, one pair of velvet slippers, one large floral bouquet, one Negro servant girl, and one house pet of your choice. The painting's title will be *Olympia*." Ah but, destroyer of my life, I told you in abject supplication that I wanted to paint a Venus and, as "Olympia" is a name for courtesans, this will only bring another scandal, and on top of it all everyone will suppose that is what you are. Precisely, responded Victorine, it will bring on a scandal, and not only will people think I am a whore but, *tout précisément*, that I am *your* whore, my dear, and in that they will not be terribly mistaken. Then she fell silent and gazed at me, full of anticipation, with those eyes of hers. I looked back in pallor. You can't possibly want this, I said. You can't want to destroy me both as an artist and as

a man. At this, my raison d'être just laughed at me right between the eyes. Just try me, Eddie, she said. I had no choice but to accept her conditions.

Now, though, everything is just as she wanted it, and here we sit in her studio (to my surprise, it looks like she really can paint after all, and, I must say she's not all that bad). I got hold of everything she wanted, and promised I would call the picture Olympia (with the secret intention of somehow painting her as Venus anyway), but still she keeps staring at me so coolly, so penetratingly, that I can barely hold the brush. Her will is done, and she lords it over me like Napoleon his Pekingese. So now what can be her problem? Here I committed the mortal sin of asking this question outright. At this my Victorine, calm and relaxed, lay back on the divan (or settee? All those words, it's a good thing I only need to dabble in colors), crossed her legs and, setting her left palm decisively on her right thigh, burned her gaze into mine, then responded in a tranquil, even tone, "I no longer have any problems at all. On the other hand, you will have that and many more. You will never be free of this painting; it will go with you to the grave. It will shape every last one of your days, and each day you will regret having painted it. All your life, you will be successful but wretched. You will get syphilis from an actual whore, in whom you were searching for me, and when you are fifty, on the nineteenth of April, 1883, they will cut off your left leg and then, on the thirtieth, you will die." After that she never said another word to me.

Need I say that everything turned out as she had predicted? They say she lived out her days happily with some piano teacher called Marie Dufour. And her work was shown at the Salon more than once.

Is this fair?

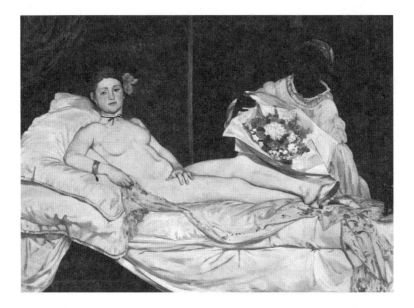

DISCUSS in your own words whether this is fair! Argue pro or con!

Physics / Biology

Bald, oder nie.

A ripe apple falls from the tree. A nice thought, mused Sir Isaac Newton [pron. "Noo-tun"] as he sat in the languid garden on a 1687 afternoon. It has a music to it, an arc, a purr. It is reassuring, even a bit melancholic, just the right kind, the kind I like, the kind you want to snuggle into and nest, that kind of pleasant autumnal thought (O, the autumn sky!), unless of course it's a summer apple, he added, twirling a ringlet of his luxuriant wig, a sure sign he was engaged in thought. At that very moment [→HISTORY] something plonked him on the head. At the time Sir Isaac's head looked like this:

Ouch! says Sir Isaac in flawless English [note that interjections, particularly the uncontrolled ones, generally leave our lips in our mother tongue]. Sir Isaac is English and, for the nonce, unrestrained.

On the other hand, a boulder worked loose from the mountaintop tumbles down into the valley. This is far from a pleasantly reassuring, and not in the least a melancholic and autumnally cozy, but instead a drastic, wintery-cold, palpitation-inducing, disagreeable thought.

Then again, the velocity of a ball tossed vertically upward decreases, stops for a moment, and finally falls to earth. What are we to make of this? Is it a good thing? A ball, tossed upward, again and again. Is this not just a bit laborious?

As for myself (but who is speaking here?!), what interests me most—

and I mean REALLY—is the *stops for a moment*, what's up with that? What happens in that vacuum moment when we find ourselves pedaling in mid-air, like in the cartoons, neither up nor down, but precisely there and then. I suspect this might be life itself. In this phenomenon, furthermore, we have become acquainted with the mutual force of gravity.

But let us proceed, no further dallying: now, acknowledging the physical nature of this force, we may say that the apple falls from the tree due to gravitational force, the loosened boulder plunges into the valley due to gravitational force, and the speed of the vertically tossed ball diminishes due to gravitational force (and we still have not even gotten to the rise and fall of the sea). A felicitous coincidence: the system works. Gravitation is in its

place, and the force is with us. (Note, peninsulas on the globe all droop downward [thus: ↓], as do flaccid phalluses, the only exception being Jutland, perhaps just out of spite. This is not beautiful, but interesting.)

We designate the gravitational force with a downward arrow [thus: ↓]. This force attacks the body at its center of gravity. Note: the part of a body designated as the center of gravity is the point at which

bodies, whether hanging or supported, remain at rest and balance. The point of attack of the female body is the womb. If the female body is brought into a situation, as it were, taken at the womb, that is, if it is suspended or supported (*ouch!* as Sir Isaac would say in flawless English, *if at all*, capable of imagining himself in the condition of the female subject—*na ja*, male physics), the female body remains at rest, in balance, in any situation. The male body's point of attack is the penis. But if we suspend the male body by the penis, not only does it not remain at rest, but this procedure elicits monstrous screeching and squirming from its subject, as well as foul language copiously cursing the Creator. QED.

However, if the little Mantegna Madonna should fling herself from the wall of our room one fine day (and indeed she has), might we say that the gravitational force has been the sole influence on her? Might we say that this force, combined with its attack point, has directly targeted the center of gravity of the Mantegna Madonna's body? Or might we not say that it is not primarily the gravitational, but the *graviditational* force that is in play here, that the preponderance, so to speak, of the suspension is centered there. [The force that pulls suspension, or pushes support, is known as ponderance, or weight;

its symbol is G.] Weight is also indicated by a downward pointing arrow [thus: ↓] whose point of attack is located at the contact locus of the two bodies. Now let us imagine for a moment the entire process: the point of attack, the contact of two bodies—so very much can happen here. Though silent, the Mantegna Madonna could probably tell us a great deal about this. Otherwise she obviously would not be tilting her head to the side with such melancholy. Otherwise she obviously would not be clutching with such despondency that

scrawny hollow-cheeked infant, exhausted from the birth process, as one who reasons that well, here we are, the two of us alone in the world, ecce homo and me. There are furrows and bags under the child's eyes, and his little hand, emerging just below his swaddling, is half-closed into a fist, with two fingers outstretched. This contributes somewhat to the indecision that permeates this image. The Mantegna Madonna supports the little head with one hand, no doubt driven by a double purpose, to hold and protect it. Her other hand falls gently on the child's belly and swaddling clothes, to hold and warm him. I can feel the warmth of her hand. Yet there is something about the two of them that will not let me rest, something that seizes me by the throat and will not let go.

There is something unsaid here, some hint, some dark and unhappy story. Or if not dark and unhappy, then something left unsaid, something that, shut up, sweetheart, you're too young for this, something that, ask your father, something that is there, since only a blind person could not see it, but whereof one cannot speak. One must be silent.

But enough of that.

No, my dears, it's not like that. Whereof we cannot speak, thereof we perhaps should try to speak, you see. After all this is why we were given this damned (→swear word from a native speaker) language,

this is how we raise ourselves above the animals, by pointing to this, as if to say, well, you know, it's language. On the other hand, when we should be using it, when there are troubles, when there are complications (Newton himself is complicated, and Einstein even more so—if I understand it correctly, this is the essence of relativity), when obstacles clutter the road, when it is time to tell it like it is ("I don't think Einstein was Einstein's real name. I think people called him Einstein because he was very smart," but hey, this was said by a nine-year-old child), when you should be grabbing the brass tacks by the throat, then it's "Whereof we cannot speak, thereof we must be silent." Curtain. Effective, no? But if we are silent at the truly excruciating moments, then who would use the words that are at our disposal precisely for such situations? That have been paid for, so to speak. They are there, awaiting their fate, and then nothing. They migrate to the back of the shelf, to be covered in dust.

Time to clean house.

Because whereof one cannot speak, thereof one may either be silent, or speak.

In England, a certain Dr. Harold Shipman, a serial killer on the loose for years who was also, and no less importantly, the town's GP, was caught because the ladies thoroughly discussed (as they do) the details of their complaints and treatment, while the men kept modestly silent. The good doctor murdered his men patients first, and only later got around to the women. This was his ultimate downfall.

But let us move on. So what is up with every apple hanging from the branches of trees? The boulders on the ground? The package resting on the table? Fall already!, I shout at the package resting on the table, but it might as well be deaf. Not so much as a quiver. Fall already!, I shout at the boulder on the ground, but it might as

well be deaf. Not so much as a quiver. Fall already!, I shout at the apple hanging on the tree branch. And sometimes to no avail. But why aren't they falling??! (Meanwhile I'm quite hoarse from all the yelling.)

It turns out, it seems that the downward force of gravity is equaled by the upward force of suspension.

Because—and this is the essence!—if two forces of equal strength affect the same body in opposite directions (Force versus Counterforce), then—well, then nothing happens. It stays where it is (apparently at rest, but in fact wrestling, so to speak).

But if one of those forces comes to dominate over the other, things start moving.

Bald, oder nie.

So if, one fine day, the Mantegna Madonna flings herself from the wall of our room (and she has flung herself), not only does that have to do with the tide, but also (so Sir Isaac) the movements of the planets, moons, and comets. And as long as we're getting into scrutinizing the nitty-gritty of the universe, how could we not place these events into their larger intrastellar context? If objects now speak to us, how could we act just as they do, when Force versus Counterforce, etc.—feign deafness to their words? Since if the Mantegna Madonna flings herself down, then one force defeats another—so far, so good. But if you're going for a top grade, you cannot but add:

The will stirs, and things are set in motion.

Bald, oder nie.

According to my notes, this is what the Mantegna Madonna, having flung herself down, said:

"Let us go then, we must make a move, and not allow Gravity to triumph over Gravidity, not allow it to act as a weight pulling us down into the black heart of the Earth (the symbol for weight: G), not allow Force to defeat us. Let Counterforce do its

work as well, come on now, what do you want—that I should beg you? Alright then, I'm begging you, do not let the iron musketball of despair strike your heart, I know what I'm talking about, come on now, let us tread the air, not fall. This will work. Come on now."

I was the only one in the room, so I had to assume she was talking to me.

Bald, oder nie.

And behold! My alembic self begins to emerge.
Come on now.

A 411-gram peach was grown in Britain in 1984.

a) WHAT was the mass of the peach?
b) WHAT was the retaining force acting on the peach?
c) IMAGINE that Newton, at the time (1867) had been sitting around under this peach tree. How much of a problem is this?

Singing / Music

Concerto
(with subtitles)

The gentle rustle of a breeze. Buzzing of insects, hiss of leaves.

We harden our soft flesh to the quiverings of summer. The wind licks at our navels: *lickings of wind*. Butterflies caress the down of our arms: *fluttering of butterfly kisses*; ladybugs pitch camp in our red and black hair: *buzzing of wings*. And hedgehogs sniff our fragrant toes: *profuse snuffling*. Even the deer, at our impetuousness, blink their eyes at arm's length: *rustle of deer hooves*. Our skinny city-bodies quiver at this unfamiliar freedom. My sister, black-maned and spectacular, prances about the meadow: *hooting*. The summer is before us. I have a hard time keeping pace with her capering though I move my pipe-stem legs at a clip: *panting; scratching of grass*. My sister proudly displays her beautifully rounded breasts, taut against her dress, to the thrushes and hares. In just one single year she's turned thirteen. I'm still only nine, but even for my sake time won't quicken its pace. It flows in its own course, unhurriedly, at leisure.

Our summer kingdom, the border village and its surroundings, sparkles in all its glory. The valley buzzes: *buzzing*. The brook babbles its burbles: *burbling babble*. The heavy, scorching air quivers, and from the intense light, heat waves shimmer atop the broken asphalt of the old highway. Our first stop is Old Man Pirka, the beekeeper. Once we're suited up in gloves and helmets like Medieval knights, Uncle Pirka lets the bees cover us. The experience is a mix of fear and delight, attraction and repulsion. I know of nothing that compares to it. *Powerful buzzing, loud heart-thumping, chuffing.* Uncle Pirka watches us with a smile as we stand by the hives like small statues with moving surfaces. Two kids in the trap. *That's the way, my little ones, say hello to our tiny friends, they're just as busy this year and*

will give us plenty of honey to drip! You can take some to your mother and sweeten up her life a little too! Uncle Pirka winks amiably; his mouth is moving. *Buzzing, gradually louder.*

We stop in at Aunt Teri's to pick up Vulcan. Vulcan will be our dog till fall. A big, shaggy, white Komondor, he can hardly contain his delight at us: *barking, yelping, panting of a dog.* He just can't get enough of us, jumping up again and again, giving

our faces a lick: *slurp. No, Vulcan, No!* Laughing, my sister tries to push him off. Big red patches on my face always betray my excitement. This bothers me sometimes, because it's difficult to conceal my emotions. At this point my face is at least as red as my hair. I stroke Vulcan's neck, scratch his ears, bury my face in his shaggy fur. My sister speaks to the dog. *Come on, Vulcan, we're heading down to the river!* We set off again, to look in on someone else.

We perform a secret annual ritual down by the river: while Vulcan prances up and down on the shore below, *chuffing, crunching of damp sand*, we teeter into the water with our shoes on, *water splashing*, then we venture out, deeper and deeper, until our bodies and clothing are submerged, *river sounds.* First our shoes and socks soak up the water, then the hems of our skirts, then come the short sleeves of our blouses, and only when both of us are up to our necks—me a little behind, but only as much as I am shorter—do

we turn back toward the shore. This immersion of ours is secret, even top secret, since mother doesn't allow us to wade so deep in. True, it's not such a big river, and the current is slow, even lazy. But still. Her prohibition only increases its meaning in our eyes, motivating us to even greater secrecy and solidarity. Two summers back, we swore a blood oath that we would not divulge our secret to anyone, under any circumstances—*clap of two blood-streaked palms*—with Vulcan the dog as our witness. Once we've emerged from the water, the closing ceremony: carefully we remove our shoes and examine what we've caught. This we call the shoe-reading, and we use it to see what the summer holds for us that year. I only snagged some kelp and the remnants of a burnt stick; my sister had a more interesting catch in the broken shell of a bird's egg. Plus a little muck. We thought on this for a good while but couldn't settle on a final interpretation. Then we set off toward our next stop, the hunting blind at the edge of the meadow. This was our own two-story house with an excellent view. Our wet clothes clung to our bodies, to be dried by the hot sun as we went, *shoes squidging*. The blind is smack on the southern border of the country, where snail hunters frequently wander over from the far side. I'm not big on snails. As for slugs, they disgust me.

Vulcan runs out ahead, stops, and looks back to check that we're following. Then he sprints back as if to prod us into running with him. *Enticing barks.* My sister will not let herself be herded. She moves at a comfortable pace, meticulously surveying our dominion, which we have not seen since last year. She tastes the ripe, sweet strawberries that melt in her mouth, *squelch*, listens to the squawking of pheasants nesting nearby, *pheasants squawking,* and shading her eyes with the palm of her hand, scans the distance to gauge how the windbreak of firs along the edge of the meadow has grown, and is visibly satisfied that this summer may even surpass the last in its

unimagined magnificence. But I give in to Vulcan's coaxing and happily trot off with him toward the blind, my red hair fluttering behind me like a flag. Sounds of delight pour from my throat—*throat sounds*—and I riot in the silken summer.

Reaching the edge of the meadow, Vulcan charges into the wood—*snapping of twigs*—our usual detour on the way to the hunter's blind. It would be enough just to follow the meadow's edge since the blind is there, as if standing guard over the green border between the wood and the field. But it would be too deliberate just to dart over to it and miss out on the adventure. I know exactly where Vulcan is headed: the little brook that courses through there, not far from the stand of beeches. I run after the colossal animal, who flies like a bolting racehorse toward the finish line, *panting sounds*. Upon reaching the narrow brook, Vulcan hops effortlessly over to the far bank and drinks from its stream while he waits for me, *loud lapping*. I catch up and take a

running start, but my foot slips on a wet rock and I twist my ankle, *unarticulated scream*. I collapse on the bank to massage my aching leg. Vulcan runs back to me, good doggie, and begins barking noisily, *loud barking*, signaling trouble, that my sister should hurry but, oblivious to the noise on her dreamy stroll, she takes a good ten minutes to show up. She examines my swelling ankle, and since we are not far from the blind now, recommends we limp our way over there so I can rest while she fetches someone to take me back to the village. I put my arm around her waist and, with a martyr's grimace, make my way, hopping on one leg. My face is hot from the exertion. We get along at a snail's pace but ultimately reach the blind. I somehow manage to get up in there and stretch out, exhausted, on the rough-hewn planks. *Vulcan, you stay here and look after her till I get back, alright?* That said, my sister sets off.

My wet socks work like a cool poultice on my tender ankle. *Quiet sigh.* Sooner or later not only do they dry out, but all my other clothes too, and my shoes stand ready to go. The sun was still high when my sister left, and every leaf on the trees vibrated distinctly in the dazzling light, *sounds of past vibration.* Now, though, dusk was falling. I decide not to wait any longer, and set out to find my sister. Carefully I pick my way down the jagged stairs and go off with Vulcan, who had been waiting patiently for me, in the direction where, from

the top of the blind, I had last spotted the glint of her black hair. There was a raspberry bush, then a bend in the path, and I had lost her already. I make slow headway on the path that rimmed the field, like walking on eggs, *noise of slopping steps.* A lukewarm dusk breeze gradually dries the beads of sweat that had formed like pearls on my brow, *meadow-buzz at dusk.* The trees cast their slanted shadow; darkness will come before long. All of a sudden, Vulcan, as if shot from a cannon, darts off and disappears into the bushes of the distant bend, *zoom.* Puzzled, I look at him wondering if he has gone crazy, or what. Slowly and persistently I make my way on the pocked and dusty path. *Dog barking in the distance.* The shadows grow ever longer, more splintery, and the horizon turns deep purple. *Typical turning-deep-purple sounds.* At last I reach the bushy bend. *Barking, louder now.* There is a shoe lying under one of the raspberry bushes. *A gasp.* I know that shoe well; it was promised to me for

next summer, by which time I will have grown into it. A pretty, blue shoe, with a strap. I spread open the branches of the bush and step into the thicket. *Twigs snapping, rustle of leaves, mad barking.* I look around in hesitation, then set off to the left, where the undergrowth seems to open up a bit. This turns out to be the right decision: my sister's torn, blue poplin sweater hangs from a branch. Goes well with

the blue shoe. Moving on, I find the other shoe and a grimy piece of white rag. I reach a thick, leafy branch and push it aside. *Mingled sounds of whimpering and barking.* My sister lies on the ground, thick with underbrush, naked from the waist up. Her skirt, hanging from her body, is ripped in two, blood trickles down her begrimed thighs. *Plop of trickling blood.* At her head Vulcan yips, licking her face, *lick lick.* I sit down on the ground near my sister and take her head into my lap. Now it's me taking care of her.

Oh look, it's Little Red Riding Hood! We'll get her next year. She doesn't even have tits yet.

Quiet, she'll hear you.

Are you crazy? What's she gonna hear—she's deaf and dumb!

Even better. At least she won't get to yammering like the big sister. Got enough snails?

You bet. Today was another good day. That yapping mutt comes over here and I'll give him a kick to knock him senseless. Alright, let's go.

Darkness falls. My face burns. *Sound of cicadas, crickets, and bugs. Music.*

WHAT is the meaning of dominant and subdominant?

WHAT is the meaning of *allegro, ma non troppo*?

AND HOW DO WE KNOW when *allegro* is too *troppo*?

Geography

Expulsion to Paradise

You're going back, understand? You're going back to see if you're
still there, or have finally managed to drag yourself out of there.
You're slow. Painfully slow. How much longer will it take? We don't
have that much time. We don't make bargains. You get back there,
and I'll smash your nose back into the past if I have to. And the
simple sight of it isn't the whole story, either. The sight is a liar. It
pretends the place is completely unchanged. As if everything in the
place were in its place, maybe just a touch worn down. You look
around, check that the boardwalk is still there on the shore, that
Christ is still around, and the bay, the sunset—check, check, everything is still there. Oh come on, don't be a dodo. You have to sniff
things first, smell the odor of rotting time, the typical scabby stench

 of the past rising from the trash cans, spreading
over the city, the smell of the sewers overmatched
by tropical storms, the hillsides that ring the town,
the smell of poverty drifting from the favelas toward
the sea and, while we're on the subject, the sea's own
smell, all used up, sniffed to death; the stale acrid
smell of mate, the perpetual mingling of the slave-
smells of black beans and rice, the smell of the sweat

of the dancers in the warlike capoeira's dances, in their snow-white garb, the smell of the bossa nova, whose cloying odor will make you ill, the fusty, naphthalene-wrapped smell of Portuguese words and inflections, the smell of Antonio, the smell of Sonia, the smell of Maria José, the smell of Eduardo, the smell of mother, the smell of the nanny—*babá* in the local idiom—the thick plastic smell of your first plastic telephone, the steamy, penetrating, early-morning smell of the high hills beyond the city, the eroding, unraveling, fatal smell of the tropical undergrowth, radiating transition, the suffocating smell of the deafening cicada-filled night, the smell of the incense-stuffed paunches of the black *putti* in the Spanish Baroque churches, the smell of the distinctive sentence structure of the distinctive literature pressed between the saw-edged pages of soft-cover books, the smell of the roast bits of beef speared onto spits, sliced from enormous hunks of beef, the smell of the secret coconut milk lurking in the

coconuts beheaded by machetes, the sticky, day-after smell of the even more secret encounters of grown-ups, the cool, sterile laundry-soap smell of the rough marble basin in the utility room, the rubber smell of the liquid rubber of rubber slippers, rubber dolls, and the liquid rubber that drips from the rubber trees, collected in tin pots, the deep-sea fish smell of the fish market that settles on everything, into every pore, every material and mind, the metal smell of the pole grip on the old streetcars, somehow redolent of death, the primeval forest smell, good for protecting the banded armadillo but unpleasant to sniff, and the sulfur-smelling breath of the giant butterflies that phosphoresce to illuminate the dark of night.

When that's done, then think. Look inside yourself. Then, if that's done too (and it's not yet evening), *then* you can start looking around. You can look beneath the crests of the lukewarm, early-evening waves, beneath the black-and-white wave-patterned flagstones of the Avenida Atlântica, beneath the patterned black-and-white geometric flagstones of your own street, beneath the giant fan-shaped leaves of the banana tree, beneath the wings of the colorful nectar-siphoning hummingbirds that flick the air like tiny arrows (whose insanely rapid motion cannot be followed by the naked eye, so no use trying), beneath the escarpments that conceal semiprecious stones, most notably the *topázio imperial*, (the stone of desire, seduction, and passion), and *água marinha* (lucky stone to seafarers that calms the

nerves, reduces fear, and opens up the channels of communication), beneath the sparkling costumes, a full year in the making, of the samba-school students going down from the favelas to the sea to practice, look at their silken, chocolate-brown bellies, look beneath the eyelashes, stuck shut in the dawn, of the armed, half-orphaned street children clouted together into gangs, beneath the marble-cool armpits of the ever-open-armed Christ, beneath the floors of the Medieval castles formed from the beaches' sand, beneath the cool, dry (and not, as you might imagine, slippery) bellies of all fifty-four thousand inhabitants of the snake zoo, beneath the surface of the sparkling sea, and down into the deep, to the impossible silent realm of tropical fishes and crabs and shells unseen at the surface, which you will never want to leave once having been there, you will aspire to grow gills and become one with the seaweed and muck, and where you will feel that you have returned to the place you belong, not by way of any decaying illusory nostalgia, but instead the bare facts of biology; look beneath the pink-nippled black breasts of suckling nursemaids, beneath the waves of primal orgasms whipped up by dolls' legs and rubbed to life by the spine of storybooks, that stone you stepped on heading to school—beneath the moss on it—look right there, beneath the raspberry-honey tongue of the secret language used at home, in the hiding place of the treasure divulged to you alone by your sibling

that never was, beneath the tremulous, gritty touch of early solitude and fears, beneath your mother's ever-accommodating body unfolded before you, and her meticulously closed soul, beneath the stopper of the little bottle of perfume labeled MADAME ROCHAS FEMME, beneath the despairingly fluttering wings of the giant cicada tied to a leg of the servant girl's bed, beneath the clumsily bestowed saliva of a child's kiss won at spin-the-bottle, beneath the feelers of insects trapped by carnivorous plants, and beneath the blanket of night, dappled with the rumble of crashing waves.

When that's done, think. Look inside yourself. Then you can begin to grasp and grope. You can touch the foot of God, for example, just barely peeping out of the bluing sea; no one has perceived its fall, they just keep sowing as if nothing had happened, the sun shines and the ships make their headway, are they blind or what, or maybe they just like to close their eyes to trouble, they like to be happy, not sad, but even sadness you learned in that other place (I can understand that you don't want to move there for good, but you must understand that you must), and it's no trouble for you to notice that tiny little godfoot poking out of the water, and given that, you might even touch it, have no fear. Furthermore (and no less importantly), you can even grab the finger of God, a blot on the center of the city—alright then, of the entire bay, the *Dedo de Deus*, Mount Finger-of-God constantly poking at the sky, the giant index finger, marking (as if you didn't know) the dwelling place of God (*ich*), indeed this is such a godly place you wouldn't even think it, but there it is, emanating from within them; they don't bother with formalities. So much so that you can even touch God's cock too, a velvety, silken, golden brown as is usual in these parts, adorned with feathers of the macaw and toucan, colors absorbed into your skin, into your pores, persisting on your

fingers, never to be washed off no matter how you try, with alcohol or petroleum spirits, but only with hydrochloric acid, if that. You can also finger the place of God's wisdom tooth: step into a blue cave and run your fingers over rocks that feel of dentition and then, at the end, you find a good-sized hole, a break in consistency, and that, they say in these parts, is the place of God's wisdom tooth, yes but I quietly and respectfully ask, now that the wisdom tooth of God has been pulled, what will become of you all, and who will now lead you

in his infinite wisdom, but at the same time, when I think about it, it's better this way since nothing is worse than a painful, rotting wisdom tooth; it will put you completely out of commission, and forget about saving the world, you can't even buy a ticket for the local train, so any god liberated from a toothache can work some real miracles, can take on any other kind of pain, retroactively even, and even the gap left by such a tooth can work other miracles, e.g.,

when your wiggling baby tooth was pulled and you woke up that night to find your sheets all wet and sticky to the touch, and you turned on your bedside lamp to find everything covered in blood: the pillowcase, the sheets, the cover, your pajamas, and in alarm they took you back to the dentist to see how such an enormous quantity of blood can come out of such a small child, and the dentist just looked you right in the eyes and, in a voice that made all lies impossible, asked you whether you were still sucking your thumb, and you looked back at him in fear (knowing that you were too old for that and that nothing they tried could make you give up that ruinously addictive source of pleasure) and, like one broken by the irresistible force of compulsion incapable of reform, you ultimately nodded, so then, said the tooth doctor in a calm, even voice, the blood will keep coming as long as you keep sucking it out of the hole, you understand, my sweet? So after that I didn't suck or slurp out anything, even when asked, and wonder of wonders the bleeding stopped, the sky cleared up, and sprouted a double rainbow.

So once all that is done, then you can start tasting and listening. For one thing you can lick the seawater to see if it is salty enough, because nothing is ever salty enough for you since the only thing that was salty enough was the sea, but they took that away from you (I took it away, *ich*), and ever since then everything has been so

flavorless that you've been blindly pouring salt on it, unbridled—to the despair of housewives, mothers-in-law, restaurateurs, and cooks, as long as there was still some salt in the shaker, yet somehow even salt itself isn't salty enough, perhaps it was only in the Dead Sea that you found some temporary satisfaction on a fleeting afternoon when the thick saline rocked your body to the water's surface like some sort of anthropomorphic rubber mattress, yes, that was a little better, but then it passed. Maybe never even happened. Moving on, you can eat out that fortune-teller woman from Bahia to get her to predict something better (or else!), even ready to devote an entire morning just to make it worth her while, anything to get a positive fortune out of her, since that's how you have to deal with those people, don't let go of them until they beg you to stop because they can't take any more and promise that everything will be

all right from now on, the future, the present—she's promising you everything as long as you stop it now, just this once, to which you mumble the following words in your mercy after taking one final, coconut-seaweed flavored lick: *oxalá, saravá, oxô*, and then you can send the Black Witch on her way all dressed in white and multiple skirts, but not until she has foretold you a completely unexpected and happy turn of fate. And then, if you can still manage it, you can stop by the New Year's ocean ceremony, candles burning on the nighttime shoreline to the limit of sight, and people pushing little boats out to sea, laden with gifts and flowers and candles, hoping their offerings will be acceptable in the eyes of Lemanjá, vain goddess of the sea, that she will hear their songs that accompany the gifts, in the hope that this will assuage her enough to calm the waves and ask no further sacrifice. The drums beat softly, as if in the background. The songs, too, are soft, and full of hope. But you—you only listen and observe.

Once all this is said and done, just pull up your tent stakes, sweet child, then turn on your heels and come, come, keep on coming, don't look back—I said *don't* look back—and then you cross the great foggy waters, turn left at the Shell station, and deny at the border that you are carrying foreign currency, and when they ask, say you don't remember where you've been, and you have nothing to do with any of it, and there must be some mistake, you must go see  your sick grandmother, which is why your basket is full of Toblerone and anchovy paste, and go ahead and ask them why they're so pushy, because this always embarrasses them, and they'll let you pass. Trust me, I know what I'm talking about. Don't argue with me. Oh yes, you're going back, and that's an order. Time to grow into your clothes once and for all.

Das Kind wird schon hereinwachsen, saith the Lord.

And there is no appeal.

WHAT COMES TO MIND when you see the following place names: I see England, I see France . . .

Practical Instruction

Self Help
(Or: The Power of Nohoo)

"Children," Mrs. Grant used to say, "life is unfathomable. But any actual situation requires actual responses that are quite fathomable indeed. You should always be able to get yourselves out of a fix, but to do that you need to acquire—anyone?—the knowledge you need. *Because any situation can be fixed if you have the Nohoo.*"

Of course none of us had any idea what Nohoo was, but no one dared ask. The word had such a powerful, suggestive aura about it that we always imagined it capitalized. Perhaps it will come as no surprise if I tell you that it became our class motto. We used it to greet one another in the halls, out in the courtyard, on the street and the tram, at the baker's and butcher's. Mrs. Grant became our hero. We called

 her "General Grant," which always elicited a permissive, kindly smile. She let us do anything (almost), as long as we were willing to use the Nohoo. We looked down on anyone who was lazy or sloppy about it, and shut them out. Learning Nohoo became a question of honor, and anyone whose behavior undermined the project was no longer a member of the pack. In this spirit, we voraciously absorbed Mrs. Grant's

newest pronouncements each week, and noted them down in our lined, indigo notebooks. Here I shall publish the esteemed contents of my notebook, which I have saved until this day. May the Nohoo be with you.

1)

Should you find yourself at the top of a waterfall, you must do the following:

Take a deep breath just before you go over the edge.

While you are in midair, you won't have too much control over events. Get used to that. Gravity is a stern taskmaster, and the water might be deep.

Dive feet first. Don't even think about trying it head first or any other idiotic way you usually do it. Hold your legs tightly together.

Jump out in front of the waterfall as far as is humanly possible.

Wrap your arms around your head to protect it. After all, if your head gets injured, you can kiss your Nohoo goodbye.

Start swimming the second you reach the bottom of the waterfall and plunge into the flood of water below. Start swimming before you come up to the surface, because swimming will slow any further sinking. Swim at the top of your lungs. Swim like a bird in flight. Swim like crazy. Swim, my dears, swim. To be perfectly clear: swim *downward*, with the flow, away from the waterfall. Now I know there's always someone who tries to be cute and swim back behind it to see what's back there, but there's nothing to see there, dear boy, just some very big rocks that will smash up your sweet little head till it's nice and bloody. Alright then.

2)

If it looks like a tsunami is on the way, you must do the following:

First of all, make sure you are not confusing this event for the ebb and flow of the tides. Make sure you are not confusing it for the movements of the stars and the planets. Make sure you have not confused the sky for a double bass, and that you are not seeing things and that your little souls don't just have the hiccups. I know, I know, a little soul can have a big hiccup, but let us not confuse a little soul's big hiccup, *mes amis*, with a big tsunami, no. We know the difference. We know how to make distinctions. We know what is how big. [Calculate what is how big!] Then, before you do anything, make sure that the gas in the kitchen is shut off, because later, when the tsunami comes, you won't have the chance to go back and check, and all through the tsunami you will soil your little panties wondering whether you have shut it off or not. This we call OCD, and it's every bit as bad as your medium-sized tsunami.

To sum up, then, if you see that the mass of water is not moving the way it is supposed to [be sure to check how it is supposed to!], for example if you see that the mass of water has suddenly become crestfallen on either side, while in the middle it is exalted like a cockscomb, and rumbles on toward the shore like a stampeding rhinoceros that cannot turn from its path *and doesn't even want to* (see Jenő Cholnoky's immortal opus *Africa*), then, like a well-prepared English schoolgirl of old (*Be prepared!*)—make sure the grownups aren't even paying attention, or don't even know what they're seeing because the last time something like this happened was 400 years ago, so then if you see there is no other solution than to rely on your own Nohoo, then you must do the following:

Run up and down the beach and scream in the ears of the porky bathers who are lounging in the sand red as horseshoe crabs, *"Mister, lady, get up, get up, there's a tsunami on the way!"* and don't for a

 minute be surprised if no one gets up, but quite to the contrary everyone just keeps lounging around and orders another drink from the floating bar and shoos you away like a little biting fly with the usual spiel of *skedaddle dang it, a person can't even relax a little anymore, even here of all places*, then you have two possible choices:

a) Just move on, inward, toward the middle of the country until you reach a place where three roads meet, but of course you, with your Nohoo, will know exactly which road to take, I can't recall at the moment but I'm sure I'll remember by the end of class, so just keep going on that road until you reach the foot of an improbably high mountain, and look for the nearest ski lift and take it up to the summit that stands proud in sun and wind, and then you will notice that your hearts are at peace now, untroubled by fresh passions, which in turn will fill you with bottomless melancholy, but then you can be sure that everything will be just fine, and the tsunami will see that it doesn't have a chance with you and will just have to slink back to where it came from and then the double rainbow will come out of nowhere and all the animals will leave the ark,

or:

b) Grab your surfboard and paddle out at an angle until you reach the point where the wave is cresting but hasn't yet started to break downward, and aim the board on the downslope, and once the crest starts drooping and makes a frothy tube, then head into it and spare no effort: ride by night, ride by day, and once you've passed Cleveland, turn left and from there, as an Englishman would put it, *you can't miss it*. Take that, tsunami!

3.

If you feel that you are being swallowed up in the vortex, you must do the following:

Let yourselves be pulled under as far as it wants to take you, and just act as if you couldn't care less, no flailing or squirming around and looking completely ridiculous and simultaneously revealing how fright-fully helpless and alone you are; instead just twist downward in a spiral like a sea snail, down ever deeper, and give yourself time to think about how things would be if you hadn't poked out little Csabi Füzessy's eye with that compass and had studied your physics like Bandi Hamza so that now you would know exactly what the dickens is going on, and if you hadn't tripped up mean old Mrs. Bauer on the stairs and then told her it would have been better if she had stayed in Auschwitz (though of course you didn't yet know what that was), and if you had confessed to Ildi Tóth that you'd never seen such a beauti-

ful girl in all your life and that you have to catch your breath whenever she comes into the room and you would do anything for her including giving her your stag-beetle collection if only she would grace you with one kind word, all instead of your coming up with the choicest nasty things to say to her so that if she wasn't going to love you, well then she would at least hate you, and what if you hadn't followed that man who gave you some kind of stamp out by the school gate to put on your tongue and you kept doing it day after day because it was good, so good, until he said now it costs money but you didn't have any, so you had to get it whatever the cost, which turned out to be quite high since you had to stand outside freezing and endure all that horrible slurping with your pants around your ankles, but it was worth it after all, and what would have happened if you hadn't even been born, and would it have been better not to be born Jewish and then the kids in class wouldn't have constantly been

calling you a Jew although you had no idea what that even meant, but figured from the way they said it that it must be pretty bad; so, in sum, you can think all this over while the vortex pulls you down, and once you feel like there's nothing left to think about and you are running out of air and what is more you reached the bottom of the river's course and your bare feet have hit the gummy mud, well then, my little kiddies, just whoosh, up to the top you fly like rockets, in a spiral just like the one you went down in, and you'll feel the pressure change in your ears, so always keep some sours in your pocket and then, even without doing anything to improve your situation suddenly you'll be up on the surface where the air will burst into your nostrils and lungs, accompanied by a bit of water that of course will make you cough and sneeze, but at least you'll find yourselves in a sparkling, sunny, summer afternoon, and the whole thing will seem like it was just a bad dream.

4)

If you see that your man is preparing to impale you on a hot poker like wild game, you must do the following:

In a calm and collected manner, take out your makeup kit and slap on your Revlon [*Grosses bises*] eye shadow, twirl up your lashes [*Cover Girl, Fantastic Lash, waterproof*], powder your face and forehead so they don't glisten like Solomon's schnitzel, then on with the

lipstick [*Prescriptives, Ultra-chic/13*]. Then you dab a drop of Chanel numéro 5 behind your ears and primp up your hair a little and, with a few gentle motions like a kitten's paw, tap the back to arrive at its final form, and slip into the unbelievably sweet little shantung ensemble you picked up at that spring sale, have a look into your handbag to check that everything is there (keys, bus tickets, last will and testament), and then on your way out the door, turn back and tell your husband:

"My love, I would gladly spend the rest of the evening with you, but alas I must go, as I have a date with the young man who pulled up to the bus stop in his fire-engine-red convertible when I had been waiting for hours for that awful #6, and kindly asked, 'May I take you somewhere, madam?' And I, klutz and conscientious loser that I am, replied 'Thanks but no thanks, I'm in a hurry.' But now I have plenty of time, and the entire night awaits us. There's some tripe on the stove, my dear, and all you have to do is light it. Ta-ta! If anyone asks for me, I'm out fucking."

Then you dash out to the stairs with decisive-but-not-hurried steps, down you go and out the front door into the soft moonlit night. I'll leave the rest to you, depending on your temperament.

•

(Unfortunately my notes break off here, because after this class Mrs. Grant never came to school again. This was a horrible blow to us. We had lost our idol, our leader, our guide. Worst of all, we had no idea what to think. Our efforts to inquire about her were met with elusive and ambiguous answers. Later, something Mrs. Grant said in class occurred to me, that it is one thing to be able to pass the Nohoo on  to others, and quite another to apply it yourself, and that this distinction would shape our lives. And then, who knows why, a dark thought came to mind: that it will probably also shape our deaths.)

Geography /
Biology / History

Mme de Merteuil
Shakes Herself

Compelling reasons and considerations, which we shall ever feel obliged to observe, compel us to leave off here.

At this time, we may not present to the Reader the subsequent adventures of Mlle. de Volanges, nor tell him of the sinister events that brought to culmination the miseries, and punishment, of Mme. De Merteuil.

Perhaps the day will come when all obstacles are removed and we may finish this Work, though we cannot consider this an obligation.

—Choderlos de Laclos, *Dangerous Liaisons*, 1784

We here present an edited version of subsequent correspondence, omitting the irrelevant passages. For complete documentation, please refer to the archive at echelon.org.

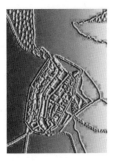

Letter 176

Date: 4 April, 2001
From: "Mme de Merteuil" <mme@spinoza.nl>
To: "chickies" <chickies@ivf.com>

I'm not joking, my little chickies! If you don't hatch, every last one of you, I'll do something that'll even make that rhino Valmont weep! You hear me? Every last one of you. And no excuses!

Your Mother

Letter 177

Date: 10 April, 2001
From: "Vicomte de Valmont" <vicomte@hotmail.com>
To: "Mme de Merteuil" <mme@spinoza.nl>

My Lovely! Malta isn't such a bad place after all, and Danceny continues to behave quite respectably. The sum I offered him on that fateful day, it would seem, has had its effect. It is terribly kind of Papa to have left me such a tidy fortune, so at least there will be some way to black-mail my fellow man if I am ever driven to it. After all, aristocracy has its advantages too, though I wish I didn't have to go to those dreadful Blue Blood International meetings, which make me simply ill.

How is Amsterdam? Do not consume too much cheese! Seriously though, you must look after yourself, and not endanger your health and serenity. This must work!!! We'll not only be duping the world in that, contrary to silly rumors (thanks to little Danceny's enormous lie), I am alive and well, but I'm actually even dividing, on an inter-urban level. This is no small tour de force, and as you know, I appreciate elegant solutions . . .

Take care of yourself, and shoo off the suitors.

Hot kisses,
V.

p.s. What did they say? Should I send more material?

Letter 178

Date: 10 April, 2001
From: "Mme de Merteuil" <mme@spinoza.nl>
To: "Vicomte de Valmont" <vicomte@hotmail.com>

Most honorable vicomte, truly you are intolerable. What are these suitors of whom you babble, for who would want to lie down with a one-eyed, pock-faced lady? You toy with me as if I were indeed your lover, although—let us be frank—this is *technically* not borne out in truth. It would do you no harm to keep in mind that you have never actually *had* me, so do not delude yourself. And take care, since one of these days I shall become furious indeed, and at the moment I happen to be in one of my biting moods anyway. I suppose this is from the hormones, plus I am also somewhat like that to begin with. Oh, and speaking of hormones: my breasts have swollen to nearly double their size, which you would certainly enjoy (the sight I mean, of course), but it is irritating to have them constantly in the way. And nothing has even become of this yet. What will happen if they generate an effect? I shudder at the thought, but after all, anything for a noble cause, n'est-ce pas? But I suppose at forty-five one should not be bouncing around too much.

Amsterdam is a pleasant spot, and soothing to the nerves, which is what I need at the moment. The people are kind (if dull) and,

most importantly, do not know me, indeed haven't any idea who I am. Could one ask for more, given my current situation? (Oh yes, one could . . .) After a time, I came to miss Paris terribly, the *soupers*, the balls, the Opera, the gossip and intrigues. To tell the truth, I'm practically dying of boredom here. Still, I know I must be patient, since this is the very thing I've never managed to do. You, my dear vicomte, know this better than anyone.

Except for the little ones, my communication is generally restricted to Saskia, the cleaning lady, who insists she is a relative of Rembrandt's. The girl is utterly insane. Good thing I managed to salvage the diamonds and that bit of family silver at least, which enable me to engage a cleaning lady, given that my arrogant servants proved unwilling to share my current fate with me. Lovely, isn't it, having the servants judge us . . .

To answer your question: There is no need for the next shipment

of material, as part of the last one has been put in the deep freeze anyway. Keep the rest for leaner times . . . or do with it what you will (oh, I know you so well), but take proper care!

That is an order.

M.

Letter 179

Date: 11 April, 2001
From: "Vicomte de Valmont" <vicomte@hotmail.com>
To: "Mme de Merteuil" <mme@spinoza.nl>

How can you say this, my dear?! You shall always be my lovely; I could easily lose myself in your one remaining eye! Whatever blows

fate shall strike—and you are its victim these days—

for me you shall always remain who you have always been: my unbearable, intolerable, thoroughly dissolute, exciting, appealing, and indispensable other half. Without you, my life isn't worth a wooden nickel, if I cannot pine after you, strut for you, brag and rave about my exploits, if there is no one to give me a challenge worthy of the name, no one to scold me to the point of pain, of taking it seriously, then my life is as worthless as the dust. What will I have to live for? And above all, for whom?

Naturally I am on my guard as far as that goes, and let my prophylactic be You yourself, O my goddess (well yes, I also use other means). :))

Danceny sends a kiss, and I adore you unwaveringly.

p.s. We went to a wine tasting yesterday, organized by the Knights. The wines here are thoroughly tolerable.

Letter 180

Date: 15 April, 2001
From: "Cécile Volanges" <cevol@kkglobal.com>
To: "Mme de Merteuil" <mme@spinoza.nl>

My dear Lady!

Forgive me for not having written for so long, lest this give the impression that I, too, took the side of those who so crudely condemned, ostracized, and disowned you. Although I had received news of everything, I was unable to write you from the convent (whither, as you know, I had retired after the events). As for myself, I did not for a minute believe those ill-spirited rumors propagated about you, which became the cause of your downfall. I had also heard that you were compelled to flee abroad, and that even your family had cursed and disowned you. These developments are simply ghastly; do accept my sincere condolences, belated as they are. I have also heard tell of the awful death of Vicomte Valmont—which particularly affected me since, in spite of everything, he was a special man of rare talents—and also of Danceny's supposed trip to Malta. I would so dreadfully love to receive news of you, if you would tell me how you are, about your daily life, and whether these reports are true.

For my part I shall mention only that I have left the convent, indeed left France itself, and have emigrated to America to begin a new life. The great attraction of this country has always been that its immigrants were able to leave behind their undesirable lives and

histories in the Old World to forge a new existence for themselves, as new men, with new personalities. After a few months of uncertainty and adversity I managed to secure a wonderful position with an international accountancy firm of excellent reputation (Kantor & Kennedy), equipped by the schooling I had completed before entering the convent. So I am now living in New York, with a nice little apartment in Greenwich Village, and a lovely dog. I am

delighting in the single life, and confess that I miss my family not a bit. As you know, my mother visited upon me a horrid psychological terror, from which I am happy to be liberated. I am finally living my own life, which will be just as I want it. This knowledge is a source of great happiness.

Please write as soon as you can, assuming you are not terribly angry with me for not having sent word of myself to date.

I send you my love of old,

Cécile (or, as you called me in those days, Ceci)

p.s. Do not be concerned: your email address remains secret, but I have a friend here who works at a company that can dig up secret addresses on the web. The person in question owed me a favor. I trust you are not angry with me for this.

Letter 181

Date: 16 April, 2001
From: "Mme de Merteuil" <mme@spinoza.nl>
To: "Vicomte de Valmont" <vicomte@hotmail.com>

My dear Valmont, you will never guess who has written me! Ceci—yes, our devout, silly, dreamy little Ceci! (I am attaching her letter.) Lovely, isn't it? Except that I was totally—and I mean *totally*—distressed that she could track down my secret email address so easily. That's reason for paranoia, no? It's crazy, no? It's shocking, no? It distresses me, no?

Our little Ceci, it seems, is no longer devout or silly, or dreamy in the least. On the contrary, she's even become a little cheeky. I only wish I had a job like hers. Though who really wants a job; so . . . common. God save me from having to do such a thing. Forgive me, I know I should leave God alone. I have nothing to do with Him. It's just a figure of speech, my dear, don't get all worked up. It's like "To Hell with Him." Or "He's as dumb as a bag of hammers." Or "You made your bed, now lie in it." I could tell you a few things about that one.

For the rest, I am fine. The little ones are settling down. Will have them checked next week.

M.

Letter 182

Date: 17 April, 2001
From: "Mme de Merteuil" <mme@spinoza.nl>
To: "Cécile Volanges" <cevol@kkglobal.com>

Dear Cécile, my dear, sweet Ceci!

What a surprise! What a pleasant, joyous surprise! I never dared hope to hear from you, first because of the convent, and then (no use denying it) because I truly believed that, had you heard of the events, you would respond just like all the others. But I might have known that you wouldn't let yourself be simply swept away by the current, and that my dear Ceci has a mind worthy of herself. And

what a wise decision America is! On that, I can only congratulate you.

As for the news, Danceny has indeed left for Malta, and I'm sure you will be happy to hear that he is well and has entered the Order of Knights. One might suppose these things had gone completely out of fashion, but no. In fact it seems quite practical to keep such an institution going as long as the money keeps pouring in from various charitable organiza-

tions. The second part of your question is trickier, as it is a closely guarded secret. But our old friendship guarantees that you will keep this secret (the way you won't disclose my email address to any-one—*right?*!) I, too, am glad that I can finally talk (or rather, write) to someone about it all, because I'm practically losing my marbles from forced silence (me, whose lifeblood is gossiping and stirring up trouble, and the like). In a word: Valmont lives! And it was Danceny who helped him escape to Malta in secret. It would have been too conspicuous for us to travel together, so at the moment they are there and I am here, biding my time, till the storm passes. "We shall dive deep and bide our time," as that Hungarian Count whatshisname liked to say every time he lost another considerable chunk of the family fortune. A real sweetheart he was, if a little conservative in bed.

I have one more secret, something I would actually prefer to avoid discussing, not because I do not trust you, my sweet Ceci, but because I don't want to jinx it. Perhaps later I can let you in on it.

Write as soon as you can. I will be happy to get further news of you.

Your loving friend,
M.

Letter 183

Date: 17 April, 2001
From: "Sir Danceny" <Keanu@orderofknights.mt>
To: "Mme de Merteuil" <mme@spinoza.nl>

Good Lord, Madame! Can this be true? My sweet little Cécile in America? I'm always telling Valmont he should believe that the ways of Providence are inscrutable, but then he always snickers at me that he knows nothing about Providence but there sure is a colossal mess out there. How can he live like that? Poor thing, I  pity him. It made me boundlessly happy to see your letter—Valmont told me about it at once, because the old fox does have his heart in the right place though there are some who have always claimed he had no heart at all. How can they say such a thing about a person? What a dreadful, un-Christian thing! I have forgiven Cécile everything, and from now on, my only desire is to see her again.

I await on tenterhooks more news about the little angel, and naturally also about you, Madame.

Passionate kisses for your hand,

Danceny

Letter 184

Date: 23 April, 2001
From: "Mme de Merteuil" <mme@spinoza.nl>
To: "chickies" <chickies@ivf.com>

Careful, chickies! Coming to check up on you! I'm sure everyone is clear about things? Fifth try, and then *rien ne va plus*! So now or never, got it? Be in your top form everyone! Stand up straight! You in the back, the red sweater—right face!

Kisses,
Mom

Letter 185

Date: 24 April, 2001
From: "Mme de Merteuil" <mme@spinoza.nl>
To: "Vicomte de Valmont" <vicomte@hotmail.com>

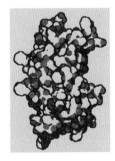

The eagle has landed!

Letter 186

Date: 25 April, 2001
From: "Vicomte de Valmont" <vicomte@hotmail.com>
To: "Mme de Merteuil" <mme@spinoza.nl>

Oh, my dear one, I know I'm supposed to understand this, but what does it mean? I've forgotten. The old brain just isn't what it used to be. Please don't yell at me, alright?

V.

Letter 187

Date: 25 April, 2001
From: "Mme de Merteuil" <mme@spinoza.nl>
To: "Vicomte de Valmont" <vicomte@hotmail.com>

You privative prefix, you Bermuda triangle, you black hole, you big big dodo, you intellectual midget, you medusa-fodder, you low-suds, Vinpocedine-popping harebrain, you!!! I've got my eye on you! Meaning, as per our agreement (everyone chooses his own conspirators), that the chickies—all three of them—are HERE, DOING FINE, AND FLOWERING!!! For the mental defectives: this just means that things have finally worked out!

Good heavens! I hope this doesn't mean they'll turn out like you, because then they'd have to be turned over to an institution. So be happy, you pearl of vicomtes.

M.

p.s. I've decided to be a good person.

Letter 188

Date: 25 April, 2001
From: "Vicomte de Valmont" <vicomte@hotmail.com>
To: "Mme de Merteuil" <mme@spinoza.nl>

My Dear!

"Dodo" really hurt. You shouldn't have said that. All the same, I am interminably happy, more than I ever dared to hope. There are tears in my eyes. This hasn't happened in forty years. Interesting sensation. Salty, for one thing. All the same, your postscript message—well I hope it's not meant seriously. It would be such a dull turn of events.

Please take particular care of yourself, since there are five of us now! (Sometimes I'm seized with the fear that we took this too fast?)

Your grateful, loving, anxious, dodo vicomte.

p.s. Yesterday we attended a tourney organized by the Knights. Danceny had an excellent showing, except that at the very end one of his teeth caught in the grill of his helmet, then broke off and fell into the dust. I told him we should just take it with us in case it could be fixed, but he only shrugged. He just left it there. Since word came from Ceci he's been catatonic and shows no interest in anything else. On top of that, he has made a few mentions of leaving the Order and travelling to America. The boy's gone a little nutty.

Letter 189

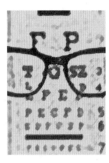

Date: 30 April, 2001
From: "Saskia Rembrandt" <saskia@spygames.com>
To: "Direction Centrale Police Judiciaire" <info@dcpj.fr>

Dear Sirs,

I have not as yet been successful in securing probative details on the individual under surveillance. Although his identity is still uncertain, I am on the trail. I ask for your continued kind patience.

Comradely Greetings,
D-305

Letter 190

From: "Sir Danceny" <Keanu@orderofknights.mt>
To: "Cécile Volanges" <cevol@kkglobal.com>

My One and Only Dear Cécile,

I have hardly been able to sleep since getting word of you. My beautiful dark eyes, which you used to love, have bags under them. (Alas my smile isn't like it was either: one of my front teeth has broken off.) I cannot concentrate on anything except seeing you as soon as I can. If you so wish, I'll dump the Order of Knights and fly to you in America. What do you say? You're not upset that I am writing, are you? You're not upset that I love you, are you? You're not upset that one of my teeth has broken off, are you? I know everyone has great teeth in America, so if you want, I'll have them done (and that's not cheap, either!). You'll write, won't you, my one and only? You love me, don't you? Don't you, don't you?

Your eternal servant,
Danceny (if you even recall the one who bears this name)

p.s. Kantor & Kennedy—that's big! Congratulations. You must really be in the money! Alas the Knights don't pay very well, though the food and the outfits are free, and we get taken to wine tastings.

Letter 191

Date: 20 May, 2001
From: "Mme de Merteuil" <mme@spinoza.nl>
To: "chickies" <chickies@ivf.com>

I hope there's nothing wrong, is there, my chickies? I have such an odd feeling. Maybe it's just this cold of mine moving into my stomach. I am worried.

Maman

Letter 192

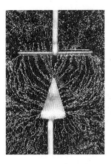

Date: 25 May, 2001
From: "Mme de Merteuil" <mme@spinoza.nl>
To: "Vicomte de Valmont" <vicomte@hotmail.com>

My dear vicomte, not wanting to worry you unnecessarily (and I know how squeamish you are about problems of the body), I have waited for the results of the last checkup. I have been feeling off for a few days, and suspicious brown spots have turned up on my—fine, I won't go into details, knowing how you despise those as well. Suspecting trouble, I requested an urgent ultrasound, and my fears were realized: we have lost one of our chicks, who chirps no longer. And then there were two, so we are four in all. I am devastated. So the kindness I have pledged (albeit somewhat casually) prevents me from ranting; I have no outlet for my rage. I think I'll go into therapy. This situation cannot go on.

M.

Letter 193

Date: 25 May, 2001
From: "Vicomte de Valmont" <vicomte@hotmail.com>
To: "Mme de Merteuil" <mme@spinoza.nl>

My dear one, my precious!

I am despondent and grief-stricken. But only think of the remaining two chickies. We *must* be content to have them. *Think positive*, as those stupid Americans say. If I could only be there to console you in person. Perhaps surely you would even allow me into your bed—alright, alright, *pardon*, I only wanted to cheer you up. So chin up, and if you must, then go into therapy and I'll foot the bill, I don't mind. Bee a graily knight. Bee a sweetie pie. Bee a little snubby-wubby-nosed teddy bear. Don't be sad. Everything is just fine.

Your loving donor

Letter 194

Date: 30 May, 2001
From: "Cécile Volanges" <cevol@kkglobal.com>
To: "Sir Danceny" <Keanu@orderofknights.mt>

My dear little knight!

For two weeks I agonized whether to answer your letter. Ultimately I realized I could no longer delay my response, as my heart demanded it thus. Yes, yes, yes, yes! A thousand times yes: I love you still, there's no denying it. It might yet be a bit early for a reunion, as

I need some time to digest it all, and to be alone to perform at my job, which is very demanding with lots of pressure, what with everyone striving to outdo everyone else to become Employee of the Year. I'm sure you understand. So I think the best thing would be for us to wait a few more months, and then come back to the subject. I have to run now, as clients are waiting.

A million kisses from your old-new Cécile

P.S. Get your tooth fixed. They really don't like that stuff here.

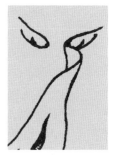

Letter 195

Date: 10 June, 2001
From: "Saskia Rembrandt" <saskia@spygames.com>
To: "Direction Centrale Police Judiciaire" <info@dcpj.fr>

Dear Sirs,

I have successfully identified several items of the target silver, but as yet I am unable to locate the diamonds. The identity of the target individual seems ever more certain.

I shall report soon,

D-305

Letter 196
Date: 17 June, 2001
From: "Mme de Merteuil" <mme@spinoza.nl>
To: "Vicomte de Valmont" <vicomte@hotmail.com>

My dear vicomte, I am concerned. My cleaning lady Saskia (you know—the Rembrandt freak) is acting quite suspiciously. When polishing the silver, she blinks oddly. Then she starts asking me again whether I don't wear diamonds, illustrious lady that I am. Naturally the diamonds are hidden away in a secret safe. But I would hate to part with her, as she is very thorough in cleaning, and it's so hard to find a good servant-girl. Instead, I will be more cautious with her, lest she suss out my distrust.

M.

Letter 197

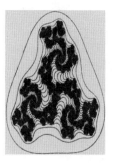

Date: 29 June, 2001
From: "Mme de Merteuil" <mme@spinoza.nl>
To: "Vicomte de Valmont" <vicomte@hotmail.com>

All that stress and worry finally took its toll. *And then there was one.* I won't go into details, as that would be too painful. I think I must depart from this place at once. Saskia is probably working for the French police. How could I have been so stupid! My kindness has made me soft in the head. In the interest of my safety, and of my one little child, I must secure another hiding place. Just as well, as I despise these graceless windmills, and tulips are thoroughly vulgar.

M.

Letter 198

Date: 1 July, 2001
From: "Cécile Volanges" <cevol@kkglobal.com>
To: "Mme de Merteuil" <mme@spinoza.nl>

My dear Friend!

Though your letter (and I must thank you for addressing me in the familiar) gives justified reason for

concern, you have made me immeasurably happy nonetheless. True, I know nothing of the ominous situation that compels you urgently to abandon your current residence, but I am delighted, and must say yes without hesitation. Naturally I will be glad to see you anytime, come whenever you wish, my door is always open to you. This is the least I can do to express my gratitude for all the motherly advice and attention I have received from you. Please do let me know what flight you will be arriving on, and I will meet you at the airport. I can hardly wait to see you again!

A thousand kisses,
Your little Ceci

Letter 199

Date: 10 July, 2001
From: "Vicomte de Valmont" <vicomte@hotmail.com>
To: "Mme de Merteuil" <mme@spinoza.nl>

My Dear, my One and Only!

How I fret about you! I would gladly repent of all my sins (assuming there were someone to listen) if only that would guarantee your safety. I can only hope that now, when you have so cleverly arranged a visa, there will be no trouble at the airport tomorrow. For the first time in my life I tremble with concern about someone. It is quite trying, I can tell you, and I hope it never happens again. (Though they say it's a regular part of raising chickies.) Please let me know the minute she arrives!

Daddy V.

Letter 200
Date: 12 July, 2001
From: "Cécile Volanges" <cevol@kkglobal.com>
To: "Vicomte de Valmont" <vicomte@hotmail.com>

My sweet and anxious vicomte (how disarming!), I have arrived safely (*we* have arrived, that is)!! Going out and coming in I slipped across the borders without a hitch, and my documents proved first

rate (at the cost of a small diamond). Ceci is an angel (I will write you from her address from now on, it being more secure), and welcomed me with an absolute feast. The dear child is doing everything to ensure my comfort (including getting rid of that mangy little dog). I take back everything I said about her earlier. She's got a nice little apartment with a guest room that I adore. She offered to switch with me but I said it was out of the question (we can get to that later).

The weather here is insufferable, hot and humid, but who cares? The main thing is that I've broken free of Saskia and those repressed lowlands. Long live the exciting, boiling, sinful city! Here I am finally in my element! Here I can finally pull myself together and start a new life.

A flood of kisses,

M.

Letter 201
Date: 15 July, 2001
From: "Direction Centrale Police Judiciaire" <info@ dcpj.fr>
To: "Saskia Rembrandt" <saskia@spygames.com>

By determination of the Center, we hereby inform you that agent D-305 is relieved of all duties effective immediately, and discharged from the Firm.

There is no avenue of appeal.

Col. H. R. Poirot

Letter 202
Date: 1 August, 2001
From: "Vicomte de Valmont" <vicomte@hotmail.com>
To: "Cécile Volanges" <cevol@kkglobal.com>

Dear Girls, my precious jewels!

Danceny and I have decided we just can't stand it any longer. We are coming to join you in New York. As we see it, enough time has passed for us to do this comfortably. Danceny is leaving the Knights, and as soon as he can arrange the paperwork (plus tooth repair), we'll be on our way. This will take a month, give or take. What do you say? Fine with you, isn't it? We beg you not to pain our poor, tortured hearts with a refusal!

V & D

Letter 203

Date: 5 September, 2001
From: "Cécile Volanges" <cevol@kkglobal.com>
To: "Sir Danceny" <keanu@lovagrend.mt>

My dear, sweet Knight!

I've arranged the apartment rental. You'll be living two blocks from us. I'm so excited I can hardly focus on my work, so I might not exactly be getting Employee of the Year. But who cares? The main thing is that you will soon be here and we can live like a loving family.

I have to run now, because I need to get to those option trades, or whatever.

I love, love, love you (and can't wait!!!).

Cécile

Letter 204
Date: 6 September 2001
From: "Cécile Volanges" <cevol@kkglobal.com>
To: "Vicomte de Valmont" <vicomte@hotmail.com>

Vicomte, I have something urgent to tell you. We have a new servant girl. She's a Czech called Martina, and claims to be Andy Warhol's niece. She tidies up wonderfully and I'd hate to lose her, but I'm already getting suspicious. I don't think it would be smart for you to fly directly to New York because you could easily be tracked. Figure out some alternative solution. I have faith in your inventiveness.

M.

Letter 205
Date: 8 September, 2001
From: : "Vicomte de Valmont" <vicomte@hotmail.com>
To: "Cécile Volanges" <cevol@kkglobal.com>

Not to worry, my dears! We've come up with a devilish little plan. We won't fly to New York, but to Boston, and from there straight to

Danceny's American uncle, a bigshot film producer in Los Angeles. He says he wants to make a movie out of our story. Malkovich would play me—a fabulous choice in my opinion. We'll camp out there for a week, then fly back to New York, and hopefully shake *them* off our trail. I know this means we'll have to wait a few more days till seeing each other, which is painful, but safety first.

We already have our flight reservations: We're arriving in Boston on the 11th at 7:00 in the morning via BA 705, and then (get this great connection!) take United 175 on to Los Angeles. From there we'll get back on the 18th with joy in our hearts, straight into your arms. I won't tell you the flight number or arrival time. Better to surprise you. We'll ring twice, like the postman (heh heh).

Until then, my little angels!

I'm so excited *I can't contain myself*!

V.

Letter 206
Date: 10 September, 2001
From: "Cécile Volanges" <cevol@kkglobal.com>
To: "Vicomte de Valmont" <vicomte@hotmail.com>

My Dears, bravo for that clever idea! Now I can relax (a bit). I can hardly contain myself either, and dear little Ceci decided we needed something to pass the time, so tomorrow morning she's taking me to her office down by the river—you know, those two buildings that look alike. She says the view is so fabulous (she works on the 107th floor!) I'm just going to faint. We're going in before 9, because our earnest little businesswoman has a meeting at 9:30. When you pass over on your way to California, look out the window from up there and maybe you'll see us waving.

Bon voyage!

M

•

Here the correspondence breaks off.

ANSWER the following questions:

1) Is it true there is "no hope"? DISCUSS in your own words the meaning of "sowing the dragon's teeth."
2) IN YOUR OPINION, if there are only two towers in Nagyabony but
thirty-two in Milan, which would you rather see? Argue pro or con.

Mathematics

The Mathematics of Randomness

Jenő Cholnoky is traveling to America with Count Teleki. [Imagine that!] They travel. They take notes. They observe. [Take your own notes! Observe some things!] Then Jenő, in hindsight, arrives at this: "The connection of North to South America is purely incidental." Pow. With that, Jenő singlehandedly, as it were, founds the field of aleatoric geography. This is 1942. The suggestion is that chance comes in massive doses, a message that hits us all square in the face. Meaning: Do not seek to lean on the rotting crutch of necessity at all costs. Forget pseudoscientific explanations. Forget theology and teleology. It's not just that Columbus stumbled on America by chance, but—*noch dazu*—America, too, is where it is by mere chance. Oh. Jenő is ruthless. Offers no way out. Continents break off, are swept

 along for a while and rocked in the oceans and then, all at once, boom. *Fertig.* Chance must be integrated into the model, says Jenő, otherwise woe betide us! These words were written in 1942. Just look what happened to the Aztec Empire. This is me talking now, in the spirit of Jenő. They mistook Cortez for Quetzalcoatl and the moon for a pizza. Wandering tutelary god, predestination, whatever. Well then

they were in a fine mess. Later, John Cage put it all to music. [Try some random music listening!] It wasn't beautiful music, but it was interesting.

One and one is two. But there are some circumstances where one and one is one. Such circumstances tend to arise through the workings of the randomness concept. The truth of one and one is two depends on whether you are adding the kind of ones that really *do* make two. Because there are some sub-cases where adding ones together gives you one.

Where this happens is due to mere chance. [It even has a name, and its symbol is **L** ([Love]).] It is unpredictable, that is, not predictable. In mathematics, almost everything is predictable, even the random, according to Pascal, who called this the Mathematics of Randomness. What must Pascal's private life have been like? [Look into it!] Personal photos: Blaise Pascal at the lakeshore as a ratiocinating reed stalk (poor fellow, he really was thin); Blaise Pascal

places his bet in the casino—*rien ne va plus!*—pushing all his chips onto Zero; Blaise Pascal in the arms of the farmer lady who is his neighbor—even he doesn't understand how this is; it seems random. Blaise Pascal is about to die at thirty-nine when he realizes that probably not all randomness is predictable (this is only faintly discernible in the photos), but there is no time left for corrections. North America, and South America: two inseparable lovebirds. What would have happened if North America was swept over to (e.g.) Africa? Well, for one thing, the slave trade would have taken off like crazy. They have taught us that the question *What would have happened if . . .* is meaningless. But is this actually the case? [Don't take anything for granted! Ask, and ask again!] Or, if this is true, doesn't this fact reinforce the principle of the tyranny of probability? It is meaningless because it is unpredictable. One and one is two. We can still somehow accept this, or to put it more cautiously, take it as a kind of order in life. But let us up our bets with a new question: one and one and one—how many is that? How far can we go with this? Is there, good sir, any limit to this? Where does it end, as Job would ask. Is there a heart that still functions, though divided into equal parts?

North America and South America and Africa—like that, all together. Pray for us.

Pakking, she says, with two k's, just like *pakkage*, according to her. She looks at me with those baffling, Tatar-blue eyes. Must have lost her way here from the Thirteenth Tribe, most likely by chance. No other explanation. (Jenő!) But what goes around runs aground, sooner or later. Negligently delayed verbal prefixes, just slapped on. Look into the sky up? Simply absurd. (Irresistible.) So then, the distinguishing characteristics of the subject under investigation are filler, wedged in between the main verb and the prefix (a giveaway, like a distinctive birthmark). High Asian cheekbones. The tongue stuck out for concentration. That gaze that burns right through you, knocks you into *eternal permanence*, as Anton Pavlovitch would put it. Fire on sight. Later is too late. In whatever situation you find yourself, always imagine you can see. I think people only dream so their seeing never stops. As Johann Wolfgang would put it. I want to see. I want to see you. Always to see. To take a glance, as if by accident, just to see what I wanted to see. Your dark eyelids slam shut, hard, like the wings of a bat. As I would put it.

Colorful billiard balls racked up on a felt-covered field, reposing in their frame. The triangle is the sign of God. This is also just chance, that is, random. Why couldn't we say that the parallelepiped is

God's symbol? Like I said. Whatever the case, those billiard balls are asleep in that triangular frame. Anything might still come of this; endless combinatory possibilities, while liberating, remain cloaked in grave silence. The nighttime moon rises from the cloud. We lift the frame deliberately, solemnly, freeing the balls. Like wakening sleepers, they quiver, but remain packed in their triangle on the green felt.

They still believe this to be their natural place. Or better put: they still know nothing. They merely exist, unselfconsciously, like clumps of lint. Then comes the cue stick and the white ball: the Big Bang of life. Spectacular crashes and ricochets and knocks and random rolling, and sooner or later they drop into the black hole that swallows them all. Sometimes a ball drops alone into the hole, and sometimes together with another. It can even happen, rarely, that three of them drop at once. One and one and one. The triangle is the symbol of God, no? *We cannot say there is no hope as long as there is a chance that there is.* (Though improbable.) Parallelepiped. Lo, there was silence, with but my heart pounding.

And then there is the law of large numbers. It says, as you know, that the frequency of heads and tails evens out in the long run. If one of them—heads, say—takes a good lead, this still does not increase the chance of tails. As Bernoulli would put it. But this cannot be allowed: the probability of tails *must* constantly increase, for otherwise all heads are destroyed, as are hearts. Rotting. As I would put it. This means that even if horrible things happen in a streak, we still cannot say that the good must then inevitably come. Things have to get worse before they get better, though this, alas, relates to another law. It would be nice if they could somehow agree on things.

Heads, tails, hearts, heads, heads, tails, hearts, hearts, hearts, hearts, hearts, tails, heads, heads, heads, tails, tails, tails, tails, hearts, hearts, heads, hearts, heads, hearts, hearts, heads, hearts, heads, heads, hearts, hearts, hearts, heads, tails, tails.

Because in fact the coin is three-sided—but this is revealed only to advanced students, once it is too late to get out. But whether two or three, you always have to increase the probability of tails, or at least make the attempt, no matter what Bernoulli says. Bernoulli should get off our case. May Bernoulli turn into a St. Bernard schlepping a cask of rum! There is no Bernoulli.

I, Sinbad, am doing a favor for the Caliph (sound familiar?), who is so grateful to me that he has offered me a girl from his harem. All 100 of the harem girls will file by before me, and I need only point out any one of them to indicate my choice, but those who have already walked off will never return. Well, experience has shown that, given my enthusiasm for beauty, the best strategy for me, Sinbad, is to let 31 girls file by,  and pick the first one after that who is more beautiful than the most beautiful of those 31. It is usual to add that, if such a girl does not appear, then I'm plum out of luck, but you can't win them all. I must say that I, Sinbad, have a few problems with that. If I, Sinbad, do a favor for the Caliph, then the Caliph should not be stingy with me. What kind of a thing is that, saying I can only pick one out of 100? What if I must have two? What then? Then there is the part about those who have already gone by never coming back. Let the nice Caliph just tell that belly-dancing mama of his in Baghdad about

 that one. Like hell they won't come back. That's just how it is. She walks off, we think she's gone, end of story, then we file that one away and have a little tequila (with lemon and salt), watch more of the series (real world), and then poof!, there she is again (generally 20-25 years later). And this is all after I've already chosen one after letting 31 go by like you're supposed to, and after choosing the one who was

more beautiful than the most beautiful of those who had already filed by, whom I would have chosen even if there had been 1000 and not just 100. Then along comes that other one, who had already filed by, and it turns out that she is also more beautiful than the most beautiful of those I'd already let go. Then I, Sinbad, am there with the two who are equally most beautiful. So what now? You can't win them all? No comment. If I might be so bold, I humbly request they put their spotted dicks where the sun don't shine. The Caliph might have 100 girls in his harem but I, Sinbad, have but one life. (And one death.) But I'll give it a try anyway. (Headlong dive in pink tights.)

Der Herrgott würfelt nicht. Unless he does it some other way. Albert, grow up already! Der Herrgott tricked you brutally. He was a professional blackjack player in Vegas until they banned him. Then he switched to another branch of the profession, and mid-last century he was banned from that, too. Actually, he was declared dead long ago, but his pension is still coming. Someone is going to have to pay that back! With interest.

My desiccated pupils burn in the hot sun. I, Sinbad, now a woman, have already shed all my tears at the peak of adulthood. Now I use Visine instead. Your thick rust-colored mane flashes in my eyes; your thick, ebony mane flashes in my eyes; the blue iris of your eyes flashes in my eyes; the green iris of your eyes flashes in my eyes, a flash here, a flash there, burning, fiercely burning, and everything comes in pairs. I have double vision like Hemingway, or there are two of everything as on Noah's ark, but alas! I am the illegal passenger on this ark; everyone is part of a couple except for me, since truly I am not in a couple; there are three of us. (This even has a name, and the

symbol L^2.) Parallelepiped. (Here: an interjection, because the meaning *eigentlich* is hiding in its usage, as Ludwig would put it.)

What is the probability that, while you are walking down the street in the present, you will encounter someone from the past? [Perform calculations!] Or that both of you will notice and recognize one another? [Break it down every which way!] What is the probability that if you invite that person for a walk, they will come because of a) Not having gotten out enough yet that day, or b) Just because something tells them to go, even at the risk of a dastardly dreary dismal demise? What is the probability that right here, something like a great, black forest will spring up, and you cannot find your way out? What is the probability that you *can* find your way out, albeit only after many trials and tribulations? And the probability if not? What is the probability that you can pull this off without losing your mind? And the probability of not?

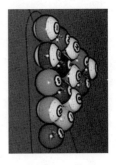

Probability analysis: (is) the mathematics of chance. It is a beautiful science. A gay science. Gay, because optimistic.

Your dark eyelids slam shut hard, like the wings of a bat.

Visine.

Teacher's Edition / Russian

On the Eve of No Return

(archival recording)

What a joy to look at your suitcase as if staring into space.
—Fernando Pessoa

Я *ЛАЙКА*. Laika the dog here. Have no fear—I'm only whispering because I'm making this recording in secret. If anyone finds out, it's the end of me. Actually, it's (*есть*) the end of me anyway but as long as it has to be, then at least let it be heroic all the same. Who wouldn't want a brass plaque in Starville? Who wouldn't want to have chocolate bars and cigarettes named after her, or have her portrait on a stamp, or be the title of a pop album—raise your hands! You see? Children, you must know the truth. Don't let yourselves get taken in, and don't swallow everything (gulp!) they tell you. And don't you believe in kiddie tales! Be good Soviet children: skeptical, sharp, always alert, and ready to contradict! *Всегда Готов!* This recording is for you, Soviet children, so you can write its message on a sky full of meteors and stardust:

THESE PEOPLE ARE ALL GALACTIC LIARS.

So here's my story about the eve of no return: *накануне невозвращения*.

I am a three-year-old female mutt called Laika ("Barker"), and before that my name was Kudryavka ("Curlie"), but some people call

me Zhuchka ("Little Bug")—or I should say "called," back in the good old Soviet past. I never knew my mom or dad. I used to wander the streets of Moscow, homeless and alone, but at least I was free. I poked around every hidden spot in the city and knew by heart every smell, taste, sound. No one on earth knew this beautiful little corner of the world better than I do. And what do you think I have gained by all this knowledge? Nothing. Nothing at all. Every day they teach you kids that knowledge is power, but they don't tell you that this is only true if all other power is already in your sweet little chocolate-covered hands. Right now I am speaking to you, bound and chained, from a tiny little cabin, waiting to be shot into space tomorrow, November 4, 1957, never to return.

Now, you might ask how it can be that someone ambling around the Patriarch's Ponds one minute, complete master of her freedom and fate, can suddenly, through the work of one well-aimed dogcatcher's hook, be reduced to a helpless puppet, a designated victim of the Soviet space program. Good question, I'm glad you asked! I don't know. There are things that cannot be understood by the rational mind (→история). So you see, it's not even true (Lesson 2) that you can learn anything if you just have enough will and try hard enough. It just isn't. I'm telling you now, in plenty of time. *Why me* is a question that cannot be answered for any situation at any time. It is a mystery that can't be known or solved. Don't ever (никогда) fall for any sentence that begins with the expression *higher will*. Shake it off as a dog shakes off water. Learn that accepting the explanation *there is no explanation* is one of the most difficult and noble lessons. Prepare for it every single day, every single hour, and when the moment comes, place it under your tongue and let it take effect. This will be a blessing. And don't you forget that a lack of an explanation is not a lack of meaning! One way or another, a story will unfold, and every story can be understood somehow, often in many ways. Get used to the ponderous freedom of interpretation, and prepare for this beautifully difficult task in a manner worthy of Soviet children!

Time passed, and life (→*жизнь*) went on. Barely a month after Sputnik 1 was launched (to the wonder of the world and the immediate curses of the enemy American people), Comrade Krushchev decided one fine day that we would send up another Sputnik, in honor of the 40th anniversary of the Great October Socialist Revolution. And so it was. The decree went out on October 10, which left barely four weeks for the new Sputnik to be prepared for launch. (→*jury-rigged*; Russian: ?)

So together with my co-dogs Albina and Muzhka (n.b.: we are all girls, so children, when the time comes, do some work on the *dzhender* problems of Soviet society!), we are being readied to be the first living passengers to be launched into space (→ *enemy American people* → *apoplexy*). Children, when you hear this, don't you wonder who will be the Lucky Chosen One to be written into the Great History Book as a Hero of the Soviet Union? Who will be the one to bring such supreme and priceless glory to her homeland? And then don't you also think wow it would be wonderful if *you* were the ones to bring such fame to the Homeland? Well sure you do,

because that's what they teach you, isn't it: the homeland forever. But it never occurs to you (because this they don't teach) that this hero, this giant among all creatures might not be just a Pioneer or an engineer or iron worker, but a female dog!

[Children, when the time comes, devote some time to the problems of unequal opportunity and mobility in Soviet society!] In fact, it is not only *possible*, but *necessary*, as you see from my example. [Children, when the time, etc., devote some time to the problem of the charred gap that has opened up between *one may* and *one must*.]

My older sister, Albina, flew on test rockets twice, on a suborbital path. As for Muzhka, they sent her up just to test the instruments. But for the launch into space (→ *orbital path*) they picked me, and

me alone, Laika the dog. I was singled out for this eternal honor, this astonishing miracle. During training, they packed all three of us into smaller and smaller cages for 15-20 days to get us used to *expected* conditions. [Children, when the time comes, it never hurts to accustom yourselves to *expected* conditions. Practice, practice, practice!] The stress caused by this ever-tighter confinement meant that we couldn't pee or poo (pardon my French), which naturally made us restless. Even the laxatives they gave us wouldn't help, only the hard training that consisted partly of being stuck into a centrifuge and a noise simulator, which made our blood pressure rocket up (*сюрприз!*). Now, don't be restless, children. You must know the truth. The truth isn't pretty, but it is interesting.

Going on four days now, I've been sitting in this structure that, as everybody knows, is ready to crap out (→ Russian: ?) at the first spin. They've assigned me two big bulls who constantly have their eyes on me, and I try to throw my voice so they won't see my lips moving. They don't want a talking dog, just a flying one.

Today, in the third year of my life, on the eve of no return, they shaved off all my fur with a weak alcohol fluid and painted iodine marks on my skin where the sensors will go. They are going to observe my bodily functions. There will be a surprise or

two. Even now, my heart is pounding like a washing machine on spin that is ready to explode. What do they have in mind, four or five days? A week? Oh please. They will *announce* this (→ *press;* → *media*), but of course they know very well that I won't be able to take it for more than a couple of hours. I heard it this morning, right from the Master himself: they won't be able to do anything about the overheating.

So it won't be a mercifully prepared bowl of poisoned food that does me in (which is what they will tell the press), nor will it be the mercifully and gradually depleting supply of oxygen, but the glowing, searing, trembling heat. Strapped to my burning throne, I shall bark the International Dog Anthem. Meanwhile, the big bulls will be listening to Berlioz.

Dear Soviet children, I am speaking to you on the eve of no return. My soaring coffin will circle the Earth precisely 2570 times before burning up in the atmosphere. If you look up at the sky, you shall see the angel of death in the form of a dog. Pick a star, each of you a different one! Tie them together with straight lines, and name that constellation after me. My name, I repeat, is Laika, which means "the Barker."

The big bulls will be listening to Berlioz.
The big bulls, if you pay close attention, are always listening to Berlioz.
The big bulls are subtle people.
Appearances are deceptive.
Deception is merely an appearance.
Good night, children.
I hope you are all spooked by now.
They will not be able to take the overheating.
You will not be able to take the overheating either.
Good night, little Sputnikites.

Everything is just a matter of perspective.

From above, the Earth looks blue-green.

Injuries requiring more than eight days to heal.

Я ЛАЙКА.

Which means:

The Barker.

Oleg Gazenko, Laika's trainer, said this in 1998:

"With the passage of time, I come to regret it all more and more. We did not learn enough from the mission to justify the dog's death."

Calculate the value of *more and more*. Draw a diagram!

Calculate the value of *enough*.

Finally, write a short essay entitled "What is My Message for Oleg?"

Choose your words carefully!

Hungarian

How I Didn't

(exercises de style: a partial inventory)

Let me tell you all how I didn't meet Anna Lesznai. I had stepped out into the garden to hoe the vegetables. The tomatoes and peppers looked decent, considering there had originally been nothing here at all. But the lettuce and cabbage were in a woeful state no matter how you look at it: rabbits, or deer, or who knows what, had gotten into them, leaving tattered, half-chewed leaves, and I thought my God, did I put in all that work to have the vegetables of my labors destroyed in one brief night, and I looked around for any animals in the area, or at least tracks on the ground, but nothing. The sky was blue, the dazzling sun almost menacing, blazing straight down onto the top of my head; I'd forgotten my straw hat back in the house. In every direction, silence, nothing but the buzzing of the summer fields, yet still I had an inexplicable premonition whose source and nature I was at a loss to identify. It hung there in the air like an overweight black raven weighed down by its thick coat of feathers, and I was sure that if I set out across the field, I would find a cut-off ear or the like somewhere in the gorse, suddenly appearing like some secret, oozing wound on the surface of the earth. So instead I again inspected the damage in the vegetable garden, my hand shielding my eyes from the dazzling light, but even so I had to squint. It was then.

Now let me tell you all how I didn't meet Margit Kaffka.

I headed out to the Ring Boulevard to buy a spool of sun-yellow thread. Colors have passed through my life one after another, like the years. The plan was to use it in my beloved new Singer machine to finally hem up the flag that I had promised to the Women's Division for a weekend demonstration in Városliget Park, though the weather was gloomy, befitting my mood, and I would much rather have been playing chess with Menyus in the warm, steaming pool  at the Széchenyi Baths, where the lenses on his tortoise-shell glasses always fog up so touchingly, but duties are duties, promises are promises, politics are politics, love is—well I'm not entirely sure at the moment, and anyway you have to occupy your time with something, convincing yourself, for a while, that something or other is absolutely critical; otherwise we would just sit by the side of the road, hands folded, which might actually be the natural thing to do—anything else is just delusions of grandeur. The cheerful bluish-reddish lights of the Röltex fabric shop glowed in the distance, and drivers, as usual, were running down the pedestrians in the crosswalk, ditto the tram drivers, slamming the doors shut in the crestfallen faces of galumphing hopefuls, all of which made me pick up the pace so my entire afternoon would not be consigned to this, and I grabbed a copy of the evening paper at the newsstand. It was then.

Now let me tell you all how I didn't meet Attila József.

I'd run down to the Copacabana to kick the ball around a little with the boys, though my mother had warned me nothing good would come of my constant kicking the ball around with the boys, it just didn't look, as she put it, *right*, since in some parts I would be considered a well-born little girl but, if I kept this up, would become just like a boy, at which I would smile and remind Mother that look, Mama, if I turned into a boy then I'd be like the tale of the Golden Stag (only backward) and also then she could stop worrying about me behaving in a way unbecoming a well-born girl, since I would be a boy, so it would all be a very practical turn of events, at which Mother gave me a prodigious slap in the face, and my dear girl you just do whatever you want because I'm washing my hands of you, is what she coolly said, which wasn't technically true because at that moment she was holding them upward, but no need to get bogged down in trivial details here, the point being that the sun was already nearing its apex over the boardwalk when I crossed the street, and the tiny black-and-white cobblestones made a playful pattern of waves on the walk, informing the less well-oriented visitor that they need only raise their heads, and their gaze, and there would lie the too-lazy expanse of the Atlantic Ocean just on the far side of the shoreline sands, where the waves just barely crested in the languorous late-afternoon light but then, as if nothing really mattered, they stopped, then gently, tenderly, ambled up the shore like the Southern Cross in the night sky to lick the bathers' ankles like so many eager little puppies, and it was here that I hurriedly kicked my Hawaiana-brand rubber flip-flops into the sand, because when you played soccer on the beach you did it barefoot, and it seemed like both teams were already out there now that Edson had finally turned up, saying there had been some kind of shootout in the favela, he always uses that one because he thinks some of us will still fall for it, so, whatever, he was forgiven because there's not  another right midfielder on the whole beach who can touch him, so like I say we might already have started except we hadn't flipped for sides, since of course it's tougher with the sun in your eyes, and so Zezé flipped the coin and all of us looked up to follow its trajectory in the sky, and right then out of the corner of my eye I caught sight of my mother leaning out the window across the road, scanning the beach with concern. It was then.

Now let me tell you all how I didn't meet Zsigmond Móricz.

We'd gone down to the station, the whole family finally together, down to the very last relatives close and distant, hazy, doltish cousins, proud, yellowing great aunts, surly-mustachioed stepfathers, generous great-grandparents, perky girl cousins and their posse, pregnant little daughters-in-law, clever big sisters, jolly, buddy-buddy fathers-in-law, ample-breasted mothers-in-law, jealous stepsiblings, chunky little love-children, miserly grandfathers, grandmothers with someone on the side, spendthrift older brothers, favorite kindergartners and gurgling babies—everyone they managed to get hold of, a gathering rare as hen's teeth. And joy was in the air: for when was the last time the widest circle of relations was together? Life had so scattered us to the most outlying corners of the country that not even in our dreams would we ever have dared hope to unite without a soul missing—not ever—and the resulting happiness passed  comprehension: not only were we together, but also could travel to a mysterious destination—and who wouldn't like a trip, who could fail to be seized by quivering excitement at the mere thought of travel, not to mention a trip so full of suggestive secrets and hopes, given that more than a few of those relatives had never set foot outside their village, let alone taken a longer voyage, so there we stood on the platform, ringed by all those little suitcases, packages, and general junk, in precisely the size and quantity we had been told, since you had to be considerate of the other passengers whose bundles would never otherwise have fit on the train, and, well, one doesn't want to be selfish, though I wouldn't call it an easy task to decide what to take on such a trip of unknown destination and purpose, since meantime spring might even break out, so it wouldn't hurt to take some light summer clothes, but once I pack that, there would be no space left for the teddy bear; best to pass that to the child, then not only would the summer clothes fit, but also my diary and make-up set—so as I said, there we stood on the platform amid all that

chaos and jostling. I have no idea why anyone needs
to be shoving since there will be room for everyone
anyway, it's just incomprehensible how some people
behave, instead of just being glad to see one another
in silence, what with all our relatives together at long
last, and share our joy in a civilized manner the way
we did, setting a good example, and as Papa always
said, a gentleman is a gentleman even in hell, well

then why wouldn't he be one on a carefree voyage, and then out of
nowhere—oh!—my heart practically stopped at the unexpected joy
of the train pulling into the station, chuffing with unhurried dignity,
then finally hissing to a stop like some giant hippo, and the car doors
opened and at last came the call to board, loud and robust, and board
we did, helping one another up with care and concern, since a relative is a relative after all, and we all settled in on top of our luggage;
I'm not saying there was all that much room, or that we got too
comfortable, but who cared because the main thing was our immi-
nent departure, who knows where, off into the unknown, and then
the doors were quickly shut and latched, and things inside went dark,
pitch-black, and I felt the train finally begin to roll. It was then.

Now let me tell you all how I didn't meet Géza Ottlik.

I went off to take a swim, as I did every day. Mari Szeredy happened to be muttering something to herself as we stood on the
rooftop terrace of the Lukács Baths. We were leaning over the stone
ledge, looking at all the burghers taking the sun. She always spoke

very softly but still I always understood what she was
saying. She told me this once as we were climbing
up that iffy staircase, where I answered with a little
wheeze "Hmm? Oh . . ."—something like that, when
a half hour earlier at poolside she said it was hot as
an oven, and I answered damn hot, or maybe yes it's
a scorcher; I can't remember exactly what, not yet
expecting she would have so much to say that day,

though it had seemed a long time since we met, so I did kind of expect it. Whatever. The fact remains that I would always give her a proper answer, and indeed it truly was hot that July day in nineteen hundred eighty-nine, as we scanned the beautiful naked bellies of the crowd, the girls most of all. Our fellow countrymen were out in force, roasting themselves on the three large sunbathing terraces at the pool, the benches and cots naturally all occupied, and I felt not the least antipathy for that throng at that moment: old men in their bathing shorts, and the young, lining up for the showers, showing no traces of petulance (indeed rather an exaggerated graciousness) and we all felt nothing but goodwill toward one another, as if it were our affection we wanted to hide, embarrassed, with the excessive polite- ness of the sophisticated world. So I was surprised to see Szeredy turn suddenly sour, stubbing out her cigarette, then turning to me. "Like I said, Magda and I have moved in together." "Uh-huh," I answered, this being the third time she'd mentioned it, and I didn't look at her, but Szeredy started in again after a moment's hesitation,

"Baby?" she said, and I, "Yes?" "Are you ignoring me?" she asked meekly, and that soft "are you ignor- ing me" here meant that as long as she was flapping her jaws I should open up my special radar-ears to one thing or another because blah blah blah, and my mother blah blah—this was, in short, some seri- ously unmannerly talk, but its meaning went beyond that and it would be useless for me to describe such indescribable crassness because the furious reproach (among other things) in Szeredy's question outdid everything else. It is hard to explain to a stranger the importance of things and the simultaneous insignificance of that importance—all those things we had ever learned together, and the crazy improbability of the world, so I grinned and answered, Right back at you my dear, and on your head and its curly locks, and you can just whatever your whatever, words we had never used on each other in more than thirty years— and Mari not even on others—that foul, everyday (for us at least, at

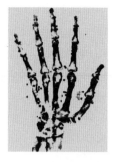 some point) institutional lingo. So that response of mine just came out like this: "Uh-huh, I know, with Magda," "You *know*?" "I heard about it," and I saw her meticulously looking my face over, tuning her ears to my emphases, though I wasn't even looking at her. She had excellent hearing. "What are you looking at?" She turned to look toward what I was staring at. "A spot is freeing up," I said, but no sooner did we start off toward the liberated sunbed than some of the quicker kids snatched it right under our noses; we should have started moving first, and picked our course afterward, "stealing the distance" by taking a running start because you couldn't tell where someone would pop up from one of those chairs, but just to go for a swim or shower, and they would leave their things, magazines, beach carriers, so the trick was to spot who was actually getting their stuff together, and then . . . but no matter, forget it. I acted like I was blaming Szeredy for our botch. "Sss," I said, enraged, "mmp." Szeredy laughed too. It was then.

Now let me tell you all how I never met Sándor Weöres.

I'd stepped out to the walkway above the courtyard to take some air on Sunday afternoon, and the neighbors were yelling again as they usually do; they must have been in the streetside room because you couldn't make out what the trouble was between them. From that distance I thought I heard just "Release my right arm from your iron paws, Sanyika, my love." I couldn't make out the response, but a few moments later I heard this: sweetie pie, little bunny, teensy-weensy. It was then.

Now let me tell you all how I didn't meet Ágnes Nemes Nagy.

I went down to the Tik-Tak for a glass of Unicum. It was closing time, but being a regular I was let in. Outside, the rain fell glumly and the languid new moon shimmered against the black sky as if behind a veil, while the blue neon of the cuckoo clock above the bar's entrance glinted off the wet sidewalk. I took the dog in with me, poor thing, not to leave him forlorn in the rain, and no one would hurt him there as they had plenty of dogs drop in, and why shouldn't they hang around in bars? Anyway I was exhausted because that was the day the new statue group with the Magic Stag or whatever the fuck it was, was dedicated on Királyhágó (née Joliot Curie) Square, and I thought screw them, here is a perfectly good square where people like to walk their dogs, and here they go

stuffing this charming thing right under your nose, this je ne sais quoi, the I-can-see-it-even-with-my-back-turned, this überscheisskitsch, and sometimes certain expressions come into my head like *by God's grace*, and Madame asked how it occurred to me to use *by God's grace*, and I just stuttered and stammered something like, well, you understand, it just came to me, I don't know how, and I really didn't, since one doesn't think about such things because if you have to think you're long past saving and the whole thing is drained like a new mother's milk, no reason to risk it, so there I am minding my business walking the length of Királyhágó Street with nothing in particular weighing me down, and the dog, for a change, doesn't stop at every last tree but ambles along at my side, and we're moving at a good pace when that kind X-ray technician from the hospital comes toward me (she's the only one I let X-ray me) because if you absolutely must open yourself up from the inside, it's not a matter of indifference who does it, am I right?, so we smile and say hello and move on and then out of nowhere I stumble onto the square—Joliot Curie Square—because it's all I have left, the best apartment I ever had, right there, which I wouldn't trade for any (and I mean *any*) amount of money except maybe for another one just like it on Joliot Curie Square with a view of Eagle Mountain and all, and then I am met with the sight of that horror that looks to have been unveiled sometime during the day, but at least it had been obscured by scaffolding while they'd been working on it, and it was still covered with

a tarp (mercifully, so as not to offend the sensibility), but then all of a sudden this disgusting refuse stabs you in the eye right here at the top of the square— pure shopping-mall syndrome—and every day when I look out the window, no panorama of chestnut trees, just this fatal error, the mere thought of which has made me so bitter that I've decided to spend the whole day drinking in every bar in the neighborhood in protest, and once I'd found some solace in my plan I ran up to the fourth floor to gather up a little cash, then lickety-split back down and out to the first bar so as not to lose even a minute, while in my haste I just about knocked over Balázs Lengyel standing out in front of the Rigó Jancsi licking a four-scoop ice cream cone. It was then.

Now let me tell you all how I didn't meet Péter Nádas.

I'd travelled up to the island of Rügen to air out my head a little after my unexpected encounter in Berlin had knocked me off my

hard-won spiritual balance, at which point I was incapable of thought and had become a stranger to my own ideas, so tremendous was the racket from the Love Parade and so, thought I, this was a splendid opportunity to finally see what a north sea was like; some people collect buttons, others postcards, others still go for napkins, but as for me, I collect seas, you might call it a birth defect, encoded like DNA, because anyone who plops into this world by an ocean whether warm or cold—the Atlantic is an interesting case on this point, because you might have palm trees swaying in the warm breeze but the water can still be surprisingly cold—will never break free of its hold so easily; it becomes an incurable passion from which any deprivation leads to withdrawal symptoms and the body begins to take on water (in the literature they call it water retention) brought on by the reduction in ocean volume outside of the body, against which the body defends itself by raising the level of water

it contains, which can result in highly unpleasant symptoms, for example if you press on the skin of your thigh, a white spot remains there for a while, and your trousers start feeling inhumanly tight; once, a masseur massaged the water out of me and I dashed out to the bathroom as if shot from a rifle, and there I made such water (make water; busy oneself with water) that afterward my pants flapped about on my legs something marvelously, but no one and nothing can massage the sea out of you; it always remains in one form or another, and it is tireless, persistent like malaria, whose symptoms can be managed but something always remains behind, some *residuum*, remnants settling nicely around the base—but if stirred up, at any given moment it can kick off that emotional tornado or whatever, which is terribly difficult to calm as it rages and slams and flies into unbridled shrieking, and there is nothing left for it but to get out to the nearest ocean cold or warm, it doesn't matter much as long as you can have a whiff

of that air and feel you are home again, as long as you can cock an ear into the air to hear that you are home, as long as you can look around and see you have come home, that the moment of homecoming has arrived and—be still my furious soul—we are home, so I pulled myself together and travelled up to Rügen as it happened to be the closest sea at the time, since events in Berlin would not give me any peace, and I thought to myself well, there is that nice little casino on the shore ringed by those sparkling chalk-white cliffs, and upon arriving I went straight there and put everything on one number, needless to say I lost, and went down to the sea where the wind was chattering, and took off my shoes, rolled up my pant legs and stepped into the ice-cold sea, then once I felt I didn't feel anything, I started wading in, hoping that it would accept me, for now I had returned home after all. It was then.

WRITE AN ESSAY on this topic: If you had the choice, which of your favorite authors would you choose not to meet?

Recess

The Miraculous Return
of Laughter

No one could understand it. No one understood where it came from, just that it was out of the blue. Where in the bloody dickens, where in the rotten tree-hollow, where in the confounded asshole of Santa, the *fledermaus*'s vegetable-grater of a willy, the oozy arch supports in the glass slippers outgrown by Cinderella, where in my creaking back, where in the crystalline-sparkling and global-warm-ified finely dripping peak of the Jungfraujoch, where in the cresting shell of the tsunami, in the jerboa's well-concealed inner pocket? No, but really. No one could understand it. We'd managed just fine without it, gotten all adjusted. The empty hole had been fixed up and rented out to someone for life. It was lined with velvet; you could putter around in there, snuggle in like a big, gray cat in the basket of a sun-drenched store window, and just let it warm your back. You could even use it for calculations, count on its not being there, of that you could be certain; this was a reassuring, fixed Archimedean point in day-to-day life. It was always laid out in front of you what was how far off and that the road up and the road down are . . . and be still my heart—and there you are.

At first we scarcely noticed. The only ones who saw were the early risers up with the roosters and the crack of dawn, and

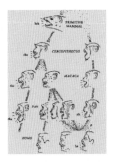

sometimes with a sweet little tart, stealing glances as the first rays of day slipped soundlessly in to lick gentle circles around the nape of the neck, the armpit and, one by one, the toes of the sleeper, with precision, all the way to the little toe, inclusively. These happy few could hardly believe their eyes, nor could they be believed by those whom they told in furtive whispers. Oh please, oh wait a minute, oh you'll say anything, and oh good thing you're not trying to sell me a total bill of goods, and the like, crass things, though these poor people were only trying to share their personal experiences. No use. Not a single one of the late risers believed it. You have to get up earlier, they were told, but the whole idea was that, since they got up so early, they saw things the late risers couldn't even imagine, much less believe. [Can you believe something you cannot imagine? Argue pro or con!] So at that point the browbeaten early risers were compelled to split up into small groups and observe the further spread of laughter; even if the late risers did not believe them, at least they could give each other mutual support. Then it all started to really catch on.

Now it wasn't just the early risers anymore. The mid-risers also began to notice that something was very wrong. They felt it while brushing their teeth or looking in the mirror, felt it when they shook their children awake from their comatose sleep to herd them off to school; they felt it when they set off to the market for shopping, and when they boarded the improbably packed improbably filthy bus, and they felt it looking out the improbably filthy windows of the improbably filthy bus. While at other times they would stare at the soot- and dirt-covered signs and see nothing at all, now the golden light glinting off the river was suddenly revealed, and the mid-early morning sunlit slope of the gentle hills on the far side; now a sort of gnawing unrest took hold of them, one they thought they could easily brush off—until they saw the smiles spreading over the mid-early morning faces of their

fellow passengers, first hesitant though undeniably perceptible, then more conspicuous as they came to suspect that something was terribly out of joint, but they were not born to set it right (whatever it was). So in their embarrassment they delved into their newspapers and tried to pretend it was just another day, tried not to notice their fellow passengers, to ignore them coolly, slyly, but it was too late now, far too late (getting up mid-early hadn't been any use at all), since that little smile had already cracked the corner of their mouths, a smile initiative, a smile cramp, a smile sapling, a smile booger, a smile belch they could not suppress no matter how they tried. All on the bus were grinning at the others. It was awful. *Nie gehört*, as my grandmother would say. Or maybe, *nicht normal*. Or something like that.

Then of course came the hour for the late risers, the *las cinco de la tarde, eran las cinco en punto de la tarde.* Actually, it was the hour of the very-very-late risers,

though for lack of time we have been unable to follow the details of every phase because the whole thing was spreading at such a pace that when we got to the end of it there would have been no time to notify the evening shift, and anyway it would not have been right to do that to them; as it is, they always bear the brunt of society's injustices since everyone thinks that if you sleep all day you're useless, though actually the opposite is true. So, as I say, the late risers' moment has arrived, and what began as a little weenie of a smile-initiative has grown to full-blown laughter making its way through the city, sweeping across it from end to end like a proper East-Iowa tornado that raises the eyebrows of even the most old-hand farmers. They didn't even have time to run down to the air-raid shelter, or duck under the table, or put on their disguises, or get their tickets refunded, or wait for the ice cubes in their whiskey glasses to melt, or deny everything to the last ounce of their vigor, or dissimulate (though there must always be time for that!), or time to make time—in fact there was no time at all, as such, since everything had congealed into this vast, hurricane-force hilarity, extending out over the city like a transparent dome collecting solar energy for a microclimatic Japanese night spot. Instantly it took hold of everything. Now the mid-early- and late-risers truly came to regret not heeding the words of

the early risers, which would at least have given them time to implement Plan B, which would have automatically launched the defensive missiles, and blown laughter to smithereens.

But keep your heads up. If laughter it must be, then laughter it is, and we shall not be defeated. Now I'll let you all in on something. The people were cooking up the idea that we'd *pretend* to be laughing, but *actually*, on the inside, we'd be having a nice big non-laugh. Such was the battle plan, and so it was. Or at least we thought so. We were laughing day and night, in such a good mood, ha-ha,

no complaints here. When asked how we were, we didn't go into our usual flood of complaints, but just gave a flick of the hand and guffawed. Every laugh felt like a dagger right to the esophageal sphincter, but if anyone who could handle that was not a fine, strapping young fellow, then I don't know what he was (and as for the girls, well, who knows what's up with them). So time moved on, and one fine day we realized that with every laugh, a strange frisson ran through our bodies, head to toe, like the wave machine at the Gellért Baths or a vibrator with five settings that runs on baby batteries, or at least like an illicit, homoerotic body massage at an all-girls' school. In short, it was irrepressible to the nth degree, and only the very oldest remembered how futile resistance was, as this was around the time of the '68 student uprisings. We found ourselves just letting go, filling the streets, squares, valleys, and mountains with it, and now there was nothing to be ashamed of, since everyone had become infected. The whole city was one great field of maple-syrupy laughs, sought out by tourists from the most distant points on the globe who came to witness this wonder of wonders for good money. Right away we had made the list, the Eleventh Wonder of the World (although as I recall number ten wasn't really anything that miraculous).

Time moved on, and the people of the town were understandably getting a little peeved at it all. Where in the bloody dickens, where in the rotten tree-hollow, where in the confounded etcetera

did this laughter come from all of a sudden? What could have caused this return of laughter, which you might call miraculous, but at the same time completely baffling and a little bit ominous? The very eldest even revealed that long, long ago, sometime before the Short-tailed Quokka's Mound-dig, there still existed an organic laughter that spread naturally, bubbled up spontaneously, but then there came the day when, sometime around a quarter after five in the afternoon in that half-dusky opaline dead time of day when everyone lets down their guard from the feeling that time has died and will never again revive—so, at that hour, as the city stirred from its afternoon siesta, laughter had suddenly disappeared, vanished into thin air. No matter that scapegoats were named (the usual suspects), no matter that people pointed fingers at one another, it was a *fait accompli*, gone forever. And now here it was again. Who could fathom this? So said the town while scratching its head and looking at itself, flummoxed. As a last resort they switched on the news for

an explanation, though only the oldest among them could recall when you could learn anything from the news at all and, *mirabile dictu*, the reporters, two bubbly, giggling women, were explaining that Little Red Riding Hood—yes *that* Little Red, beloved of us all—had finally become pregnant with the Wolf's baby, and even Grandmother had forgiven her that thoroughly unacceptable, disgraceful *mésalliance*, so

now the übercool little family was overjoyed at the approaching birth of little Bitty (as long as its mother's name was a diminutive, the baby's name was to be doubly that—such was the ancient rule that everyone tended to follow).

And so this unexpected turn of events directly (and, obviously, in retrospect) precipitated the miraculous return of laughter.

Now if you all hadn't laughed so much—I'll make you sit apart— my story could have continued.

1) DRAW an alternative family tree! Compare and contrast which of yours has thicker and deeper roots, then try to explain why this is a good thing!

2) MAKE UP mathematical problems where the sum of laughter is constant!

3) AND FINALLY, you in the back, TELL ME what's so funny, so we can all laugh along!

A Vast Rift in
the Great Joy of Being

(Afterword to the German translation of Night School*)*

by Péter Nádas

Not that she is aloof, or that she conceals herself dallying in role-play but, all the same, she is one of those authors whose work does not follow naturally from their autobiography. Her confidence is formidable: She was laid down like a cornerstone at the moment of her conception. For all she cares, the winds can blow, the freeze set in, the rain pour down. Her perspective is impartial and free of self-satisfaction, and why should she need any? She is inquisitive—a little but not too much—but her curiosity has real determination, with no need to elbow its way forward. In fact, she does not really even have a subject. No: she has a great many subjects. Everything is her subject, or anything *might* be her subject, including things she has never encountered. Whatever the case, the literary subject is not something an author ponders, but instead stalks and hunts it down. It steals in from the shoreline, singling out the author, unchosen; leave the thinking to the researchers. If I read her right, she feels that knowing everything is not worth the candle, though her objective knowledge is extensive, her background understanding profound and precise. Yet she still sees no problems as such, either ones she wants to solve, or ones she doesn't, whether social or esthetic problems, or even ethical ones. And her language is free of problems most of all.

Though her mother tongue is Hungarian, as are her writings, her first language was Portuguese, followed by all the rest. But for her, the world is more than a complex of problems—not that she steers clear of confrontations. Her own conscience is replete with them. It bypasses the surface to delve, to investigate forms of manifestation. These are her stock in trade. For me she is a thin-walled glass swelling at the brim with water. I could not begin to pigeonhole her figures with one label or another, to describe her women one way, her men another. Rather they are creatures with fairy-tale attributes, and generally molded to their own advantage. There is some irony in all this, even occasional scorn, and exaggeration in the service of her descriptions, but no actual judgment, no didactic purpose or critical edge. One thing is certain: There are a great many of these fairytale figures, all distinct from one another. They emerge in quick focus within the narrative space and then, even more expressively, take on their own distinctive shape, as if she sees many people in one. She singles out one with her somewhat curious eye, then envisions all the others who live within that one. Not explicit about their similarities and differences, she instead informs us of both simultaneously, in her distinctive fairy-tale tone, perceiving their manifold nature through the experience of individual forms, creating her language in the service of this multiplicity which, for her, is no swarm or crowd or faceless mass. All is part of a larger surge: words, figures, shapes, desires, and decisions, now thwarted or delayed. Sometimes a mere momentary glance is held up, then flows over the obstacle and gurgles onward. She must be mindful of fluid dynamics as she writes. While creating the effect of ideas forming on the fly, through arrhythmic jumps and free associations flashing their way carelessly into the world, her every gesture is actually closely controlled, fully scrutinized. So her characteristically incompatible contradictions give us, as we read, something akin to pain.

Emotional forms clash with forms of thought; literary conventions dissolve in her hands. She is a poet and philosopher, bound up crosswise, a pair of her own opposites. Were her textures not so imbued with forms of thought, you might say she was writing prose poetry (or the converse); if a single one of her characters were not so imbued with the forms of emotion, you might call her a philosopher of emotions. Assuming there is such a thing. If there were such a thing.

There are things in Heaven and Earth that even the most pedantic philological minds cannot untangle into strands and arrange. But she herself is arranged, concrete, objective, free of generalization, and watches her characters in close-up. As for the events, and their flows and shifts, that provide a foundation, her perspective is only half-close-up, for she would never impede their unfolding or impose restrictions. On the other hand, experience is a vivid presence in her rear-view mirrors. And experience always puts the brakes on prose, as it involves memory; her own embraces both historical and cultural forms, and what is more, conscious and unconscious are very much in sync in her writing. I imagine, while reading her, that her eyes are on everything, but also somehow look outward, in every direction, like whirling mirrors out in the Nevada desert—or in her textual space. Her proliferating images sometimes project atop each other in asymmetrical order. Zsófi Bán (I use her nickname intentionally) stands at the edge of wisdom. Though I hesitate to say it outright, she might be a truly wise owl. Fortunately for us, her wisdom is never forced, nor does she have any use for didactic morals except to make fun of them. The world, for her, teems with knowable things. Naturally with her wide-ranging scholarly background she sees them in their historical, linguistic, and cultural forms alike. Even so, she does not write about them, or explain them, or deny or deconstruct them. Instead, her narratives are written *in between* them, so to speak. She almost physically wedges her way in. Her every sentence amounts to naming those intervening gaps, giving reports, and documentation from the borderlands. Were she not so enduringly light-hearted, this would all likely clash with her unconventionality.

Reading Zsófia Bán is just plain good. "Enjoyable" is the first word that comes to mind for me. She leads us through a series of delights with her fabulous lightness of mind and biology; we follow her footsteps in breaking through the thorny bush of enjoyment. She leads us into great enchanted forests of joy that, it turns out, have no exit. Another good thing: you can't see known worlds from there. The unknown is not fearsome since its discovery leaves no unpleasant heroic aftertaste. Even so, there is no version of Hungarian so empty of masculine bravado—not in the sense that such a language never existed and Zsófi Ban came along and invented it; rather, it is so singular, so special, so filtered of all that is personal and autobiographical. Yet even so, aspects of individuals are on such parade here that in principle it should be impossible to offer anything at all in the way of literature. This can only work because she is writing about the *no-such-thing* in the language of *cannot-be*—in other words, her language is a perfect fit for her subject. She thinks while she sings and sings while she thinks, so when a whole fairy-tale village sets to looking for its Ur-mother, motherwhere (no-such-thing) without actually finding her, the experience is agreeably disquieting.

Reading the German translation is like reading Hungarian, or as if she'd written it in German to begin with. I sense this when I feel that usual delight in a smile that forms on my face on its own. The text is so forceful that right away it rearranges your facial musculature. The German version has the same effect as the original. The conclusion would be that this kind of joy, if it manages to break through into a foreign language, must be more powerful than the mother tongue itself. It needs to cross closely-guarded geographical borderlines without impediment. Zsófi Bán writes her stories into the interstices between known worlds, yes, but also enters into the gaps between languages themselves; no need to force them open. The Bán smile will show up on the face of every last reader, sometimes it breaks out into a shrill cackle, like a volcanic eruption, raw, explosive, blasting the lava neck out of its millennial cone. Less often, it turns to shock, darkness, gloom, and the sudden recognition of tragedy.

Then the summer landscape returns, swaying to gentle breezes as if nothing *had* happened. Or if something had happened, the world and its ceaseless proliferation have already covered it up, woven it shut, drowned it; things bubble on, effacing all tragedy. Throughout this unending smile from her learned yet happy, biting yet playful, and most of all, raw texts, you stop and ask *For God's sake, where are we now?* Not where am *I*, but where are *we*? What region, at what time? Where are we headed in these texts, with our feet, but also with our minds? Do I have an answer? It's not so simple, and probably follows naturally from her own biography.

The village crying out for motherwhere is a place that puts a name on the most searing gap imaginable, the source of our very pleasure in life, which everyone in the village views as his own origin, and also immediately feels the trauma of its loss, goes mad from it, indeed finds himself tyrannized by it—the gap itself is the tyrant—is no Hungarian village. Not a bit. This despite the fact that Bán offers what is the Alpha and Omega of life in every conceivable community: the lost Ur-mother whom every man and woman carries within themselves, an emotional form experienced, to the very end of life, as a loss. This encompasses the tribal and national, and familial, and the warmth of the familiar nest cradling the individual, the most personal symbols and gestures. These can be reshaped through the lens of the individual or community, through rituals or, as we sometimes call them, neuroses. We do not know how we ended up here in this emotional space where Zsófia Bán was born and raised to the age of eleven, but know that we are, at least a little bit, in South America. It would be difficult to locate Bán's writing in the scheme of familiar models. Pedro Paramo's village came first to my mind. She is far from the raw, bony style and somber mood of Juan Rulfo, though similar in her ritualistic conception of life. Those great South American writers inspired by Juan Rulfo know no motherwhere-type villages, or anyone like Motherwhere herself. Even so we have no trouble seeing what the writers of that distant continent recognize as their own: the substance of their rituals, their social structure, aura, aroma, rhythms, identity and mood, network of relationships, their family-centrism, and the special language of their vegetation. This is the voice of a determined anti-Wittgenstein who balances the joy of conventional language, of forms of perception, of logic, of image and object, of shaping, following, portrayal, and miming, in short, sets the joy of forms of thought and esthetic observation against silences both voluntary and imposed. As she herself writes: "No, my dears, it's not like that. Whereof we cannot speak, thereof we perhaps should try to speak, you see. After all this is why we were given this damned language, this is how we raise ourselves above the animals, by pointing to this, as if to say, well, you know, it's language." Later she would become an Americanist, author of numerous scholarly works, a university professor who would once again examine, through the lens of that special field, her own birthplace and the European setting of her adulthood. The resulting refractions are dazzling.

Zsófia Bán grew up in Brazil and Hungary, and is the author of two works of fiction and four essay collections. She's won the Glass Marble Prize, Tibor Déry Prize, Palládium Prize, Mozgó Világ Prize, Attila József Prize, and Balassa Péter Prize for her writing. A former writer-in-residence at the DAAD (German Academic Exchange Service) program, she is currently a professor of American Studies at Eötvös Loránd University in Budapest.

Jim Tucker, a classical philologist living in Budapest, translated works from German, French, and Italian before making the acquaintance of George Konrád, for whom he has since translated some 35 essays from the Hungarian, in addition to works by numerous other authors.

Péter Nádas is one of Hungary's greatest authors, and has had seven volumes translated into English, including *A Book of Memories* and *Parallel Stories*.

**OPEN
LETTER**

**OPEN
LETTER**

WWW.OPENLETTERBOOKS.ORG